THREE MEN & A STRANGE MURDER

A THOUGHT PROVOKING CRIME THRILLER MURDERING MINDS BOOK 2

CHITRANGADA MUKHERJEE

Copyright © Chitrangada Mukherjee
All Rights Reserved.

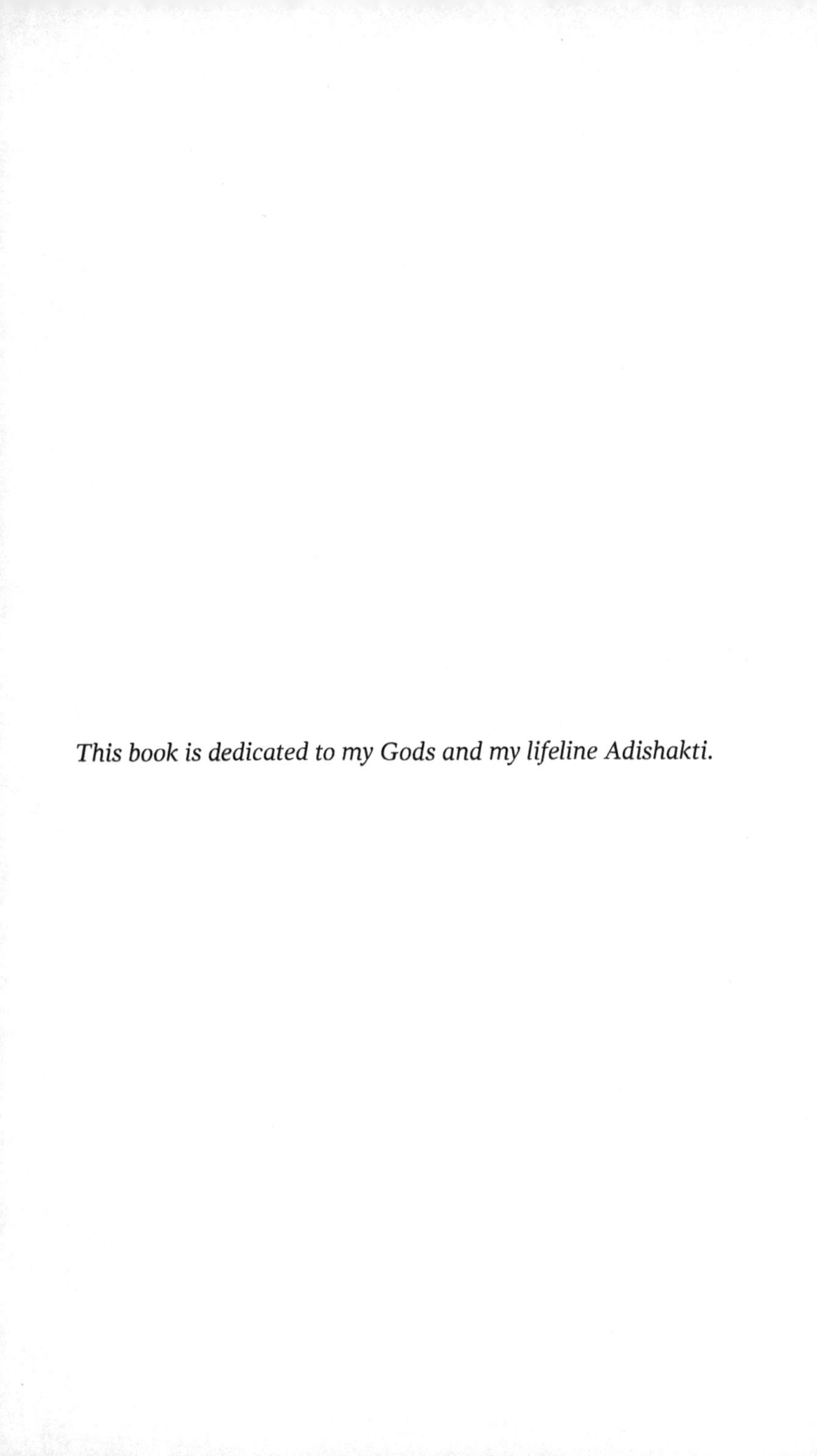

This book is dedicated to my Gods and my lifeline Adishakti.

Contents

Contents

Contents

Acknowledgements

Thanks to all of you who have helped during the creation, edit, and review of the book.

Review Highlights

"Gripping and lucidly written, this is the work of an accomplished storyteller."
 - Mujibur Rahman, Scholar, Columnist and Critic

"Narrative is the big winner of this novel. The language is simple yet classic. I read the diary alone twice."
 - Ashok Subramaniam, Poet & Author

"This novel is not only a ruminative thriller with a strong subtext but it's also a layered murder mystery that aims at conveying powerful socio-academic messages without turning preachy. Or, without compromising on the thrill of a thriller."
 - Debolina Mukherjee, Teacher, Educator

"Chitrangada's language skills are extraordinary and she holds the plot very well."
 - New Asian Writing

"Here's a book that blurs the boundary between fictional crime and true crime with a starkly imaginative and intelligent plotline."
 - Deepan Maitra, IITian, Bibliophile, Reviewer

Note To The Reader

This crime novel is about a murder and the dissection of it.

It's also about certain social, academic and neurological issues, which have been painted with a poignant brush.

Not to forget that this psychological thriller is an up, close and personal look at the complex terrain of the human mind and an endeavour at exposing its many shades.

With this book, we see the rise of **Inspector Jui Roy** and her partner in solving crime, Sub Inspector **Pritam Das.**

बुरा जो देखन मैं चला, बुरा न मिलिया कोय ।

जो दिल खोजा आपना, मुझसे बुरा न कोय।।

कबीर दास

Translation:
"When I looked for evil, I couldn't find any. When I searched my heart, I discovered that I am the biggest of all evil."
Kabir Das
"Without the color, I don't know how to proceed. I'm lost in shades of gray."
— Wendy Mass, A Mango-Shaped Space

CHAPTER I

Rituparna's Diary

21 November, 2018

I've not made my entries by date. Instead, I've been doing it monthly. Truth be told, I don't even have a proper diary. Converting an old ruled notebook, albeit a long one into a diary seemed like a good idea.

To add a touch of nicety, I've covered it with red and white Christmassy wrapping paper. I am not sure how I came upon this festive paper.

Was it a gift from a student?

Or from someone distant that my mind chose to delete in a hurry?

The wrapping paper has a distinct flavour of an old book dunked in homemade chocolates and hidden away in a cupboard next to mothballs. Maybe a box of chocolates was sent in it from someone unremarkable but pleasant. Or, a maudlin romance penned by a name I've never heard of.

The wrapper takes my mind off everything. For a moment, I lose myself in its warm colours and fragrance. Although I fail to recollect the face of the one who gifted me this delightful and luminescent piece of paper, it does balm my jingling nerves.

I have always prided myself on the strength of my memory; the blinding speed with which my brain reproduced facts and dry data. Until a week ago, I was perfectly capable of recalling everything I had wanted to. I can't claim so anymore because in the last few days, my world has turned topsy-turvy. The debilitating dread that has come to keep me company doesn't let me rest.

A loud knock on the door hurls me hard on the ground of reality. I don't want to open the door. These days, a dim sound or a harsh cacophony unleashes a howling hyena in me. The entity at the door rings the bell this time. Instead of knocking.

Cautiously, I pick up the old axe with a long wooden handle and a lacklustre blade that I had stumbled upon in a cobwebbed corner of this home when I had first moved in. I had even joked about it, "A morbid housewarming present from a morose house owner."

The axe has been useful to till the soil and to plant red roses. Some of the roses bloomed on the day of purchase, a few bloomed a day or two later and the rest haven't bloomed yet. I fear they might not. Not all that's nurtured blooms. The bell rings again. Several times. Agitation written all over its jagged sound. Stepping into the living area, which is right next to my bedroom, I wait. The bell stops ringing. This time he calls out my name timorously. I am no stranger to the tenor of his voice – the familiar staccatos and legatos.

I drop the axe.

He pounds on the door, pleading my name.

Instead of opening the door and letting him in, I go back to my bedroom and date my entry.

CHAPTER II

The Corpse

On the second day of 2019, right after the revelry of welcoming a new year had started to fade, the laughter of a much-in-love couple filled the precincts of Banamalipur with mirth. The Dutta's were delighted to have found their love nest. After searching for days, Amrita Dutta, the petite, dusky and giggly bride had been informed through a friend about this cottage-like house, right next to a private school, which was vacant and ready for occupation.

"We are going to turn this place into our home." She beamed. Her smile warming up the misty coldness of the morning as her reticent husband Bimal watched from a distance. She ran her eyes over the small living room, which with effort would be transformed into a snug and bright living space. "We don't have to buy a sofa set." She smiled at her husband who had just joined as the transport manager at the Rainbow School. The posh private school with a reputation of charging exorbitant fees and producing bright but irreverent students.

"We can—" "No, no. We don't," Amrita protested. "All we need are some plants and a bright couch. I am thinking mauve or an electric blue. You know it will do wonders to this room..." Her voice trailed off as the loud cry of their dog Kuttush was heard from outside the house.

"Why is he wailing?" Amrita stared at her husband in surprise. She had never heard the happy animal bawl.

"I did feed him in the morning," Bimal mumbled taken aback. He was a keen observer and he knew his dog, like nobody else.

3

When the wailing got louder, together they ran out. Their one-and-a-half-year-old German Shepherd continued to howl and dig furiously in the empty patch at the back of the house.

"What happened, sweetie?" Amrita cooed. She had fallen in love with Kuttush the moment she had seen him walk in regally with Bimal who had come in with his parents to fix a date for their wedding.

Bimal had tagged Kuttush along as he had wanted his life partner to accept and love the two-foot canine – the way he did. And Amrita had warmed up to the large but genial animal in no time. "He is agitated." Bimal scrunched his eyes stepping closer to his dog, which was digging into the ground with an eerie vigour. Amrita stood in silence feeling uncomfortable. There had been only a few occasions in which she had found herself speechless. She didn't like it that this was turning out to be one of them. Ambling towards the centre of the large backyard, Bimal squatted next to his beloved dog.

"What is it, Kuttu?" He whispered more to himself than to the animal which was singularly focussed on delving into the dark brown patch of soil with no grass or vegetation on top of it.

Hours later, as the husband and wife watched in horror, a partially decomposed body of a woman emerged in front of their eyes beneath the soil. Kuttush wagged his tail and licked his master hoping for a reward but the glowing bride who until now had been delighted at having found a cosy love nest collapsed on the ground, her glazed eyes open, with a look of stupor on her face.

CHAPTER III

Rituparna's Diary

December, 2017

This is my first entry. Do I even have to write this? Isn't it obvious? I am writing on the second page of this notebook. We have been taught to leave the first page blank. Maybe because unlike life, in a diary, you can change the beginning.

I only wish that I have the strength to edit my ending. I don't like dates. I love numbers but I detest dates. Why anyone should put numbers to a warm, glorious day or plaster digits to a gloomy, temperamental night has always s puzzled me?

Dates are nothing but a vulgar stamp on an invaluable moment, a dilution of colours in an otherwise gorgeous painting. I am not going to number my entries. Anne Frank did because she knew her days were numbered.

I am a diehard optimist hence I will journal my days in Agartala in months. This is my first month in this small, quaint, laid-back town and I've already found a lovely, little house to stay in all by myself.

Many might think of it as a bad idea. A single young woman living alone in an unknown city. Safety might be their foremost concern. To them, I must declare, I do have an inanimate axe, which I'll wield as a weapon if the need arises.

I did contemplate about keeping a growling canine. The more I thought of it, the better it got of me and eventually, I had to discard the idea. The upkeep of a new being is not my cup of tea. I am in no state to take care of anyone, but myself. And solitude...?

Well, it doesn't frighten me. It's rather an old friend. I've lived alone for as long as I can remember. After my parent's death, my divorcee aunt adopted me. She was not good with exhibiting emotions and made no particular effort to change. Even in the presence of a five-year-old child.

Maybe, I didn't warm her heart enough and reflected her frigid exterior at her. In my aunt's tiny apartment right atop a narrow lane in Jadavpur, I began inhabiting an isolated world filled with magnetic numbers.

Figures intrigued and fascinated me. The more I learned what in school was termed as Mathematics, the more I wanted to comprehend and befriend it. My peers and teachers were in awe of my ability to interpret and decipher complex sums and equations. Their warm appreciation blanketed my otherwise cold childhood.

Although I grew up loving Maths, I couldn't understand the workings of the heart. Studying life sciences and psychology did provide clarity on why the brain did what it did, but I couldn't for the life in me understand that abstract emotion of love. It was chemicals and hormones the books said, but what about the poetry that was born out of it? The anguish that bristled for days.

The yammering in your shattered insides when you found your first unrequited teenage love in the arms of a fickle but attractive someone -- with no appreciation for numbers or poetry. To resolve this cryptic puzzle, I ventured into the world of English literature. Reading Chaucer, Byron, Shelley, Keats, Shakespeare and the like made me realise what my aunt never expressed or my friends never confided – love wasn't easy to deconstruct. With every poem and tale, it only transformed into an arcane enigma.

After paging through innumerable books over the years, I didn't succeed in understanding love but I did fall in love with English literature and its myriad hues. When it came to choosing a subject for college, I opted for my first love Mathematics and did a Master's in it. Later, I did a Master's in my second love English through distance education.

I wanted to study further and garner a doctorate in Mathematics but then, life intervened. The man I had loved and married betrayed my trust and I had to escape to a place where no one knew me. When a friend at college mentioned an opening in the far flung city of Agartala, where a large chunk of the population comprised of Bengalis, I saw it as a perfect solution to a perplexing theorem.

In search of solace, I travelled to an unknown city. With the hope that with time and distance, I'll string back the broken pieces and make a Kintsugi out of my bruises.

CHAPTER IV

The Investigation Begins

Inspector Jui Roy was drinking her third cup of tea and tapping her fingers on the file of a case that was about to be resolved.

While she pored over the pages of the insipid case, the culprits were being nabbed in distant Dharmanagar. She had rung up Inspector Rimbai of the Dharmagar police station and informed about the three young criminals who had been wreaking havoc in the homes of unsuspecting residents in the capital for the past six months. They had given the West Agartala police a slip and gone into hiding in Dharmanagar, the biggest town in North Tripura.

"We will get them before they cross over to Bangladesh. Don't worry." Her colleague and friend assured her.

"Thanks. I really can't afford to lose more goons to our neighbour."

"You won't. By the way, congratulations! You are in the big league now." Rimbai chirped.

"It's not official, yet. How did you find out?"

He burst into laughter. A strange habit or not, Renzel Rimbai laughed loudly, whenever he could. Despite life and its countless complications, he never waited for an opportunity to laugh. He seized one when he felt like it. "You have no confidence in your old friend, do you? News in the department reaches me first. Always. Ha...ha...ha."

Inspector Roy smiled faintly, some of his bonhomie rubbing on her too. "I've always wanted to be in homicide. Since my training at the KTDS Academy--"

"I know, I was there with you." He cut in giggling. "Anyway, what I need is lunch at your home. Ask *Kakima* to make her *chingrir jhal* and her lip-smacking *shutkir chutney*." He said in his loud voice. She could still perceive his laughter on the phone.

"I will." She promised. If there was one person Inspector Jui Roy liked talking to, it was the tall, fit, rose cheeked and affable Rimbai. They had become fast friends during their days at the police training academy. With him, she always let her guard down.

"And Happy New Year, Roy!"

"Happy New Year! I thought we were past these formalities."

"Don't try to cover up. You forgot to celebrate New Year and concluded that the world did the same."

He wasn't wrong. Eating piping hot *katla* fish curry with aromatic, small-grained *khasher* rice in the silence of her home, sitting next to her taciturn mother couldn't be counted as a New Year bash.

"Do give my regards to SP Roy. How is he doing? Haven't seen him in ages."

Grunting, she murmured, "Got to go," and hung up before Rimbai could probe further. Although she knew that his intention was not to remind of her illustrious uncle or spite her -- the bitter truth was that she didn't like to be tagged to him.

In the beginning, as a young recruit, she had taken pride in the achievements of the honest and brilliant police officer and her mother's younger brother. But, with time the euphoria and pride had been replaced by the pressure of living up to the expectations of a man who didn't have to fight out the inherent sexism in a pro-male job.

Although SP Roy had retired after the Sukanto Bhattacharjee case, which was closed due to lack of evidence, he was still revered in the police circle. No one cared that his final case had been a failure. Everyone was still in awe of her *Mama*, who during his tenure as the SP had rendered Agartala safe and secure for its people. With time, the baggage of her lineage had turned into plain disdain for the man who had never been anything but a mentor and an affectionate uncle.

Snapping out of the unpleasant reminiscence, she focussed on the case file. It needed a final entry and she was positive of closing it by tomorrow. Tossing the new file over rows of old and new files, which along with the stacked papers occupied most of her large wooden desk, she sprang up from the brand new ergonomic chair. It was time for another cuppa.

Stretching her arms and rotating her neck clockwise and anticlockwise – ten times – a daily ritual, she picked her mobile phone and stepped away from her tiny room, which had been her workplace for the past three years.

"Ma'am, SP Yadav wants to meet you." A shrill voice made her almost jump.

"Don't sneak up on me. How many times have I told you that, Riang?" She hissed glaring at the reed thin recruit.

"Sorry, ma'am. He wants to meet now." The young, tribal, clean shaven constable who resembled a school dropout reiterated with no sign of remorse on his face.

Inspector Roy followed the lanky fellow with a frown. She didn't like to be disturbed when she had tea on her mind. When her husband of two years, Raghav had walked out of her life, a year ago, exactly on this day, she had drowned her grief in countless cups of tea. Her frazzled mother despite her reservations hadn't stopped her daughter from giving in to the addiction.

"She adds milk and sugar. And ginger. It's therapeutic." Mrs Roy had said to her maid when the latter had expressed her anger at having to make about ten cups of tea every day. Without any raise in her salary.

Mrs Roy on the other hand was relieved to note that her only child had chosen tea over alcohol and drugs. After all, the English tea with a large chunk of ginger couldn't possibly harm a young woman of twenty eight.

"Sir." Inspector Roy saluted standing ramrod straight in front of SP Yadav. Her observant eyes fell on the wooden desk of the SP, which due to daily cleaning by the housekeeping staff appeared spic and span. There was a cane photo frame on his desk. It wasn't there earlier. Two happy kids and a seemingly cheerful and pretty wife smiled at her. The photo frame faced the door, not the SP. It did appear that it was meant for visitors and passers-by rather than for the man sitting next to it.

"Your salute isn't rusty, yet." SP Prakash Yadav said in his baritone. The honest and industrious IPS officer had served in almost all parts of India and had been recently posted to the tiny north-eastern state.

Transfers were a big part of his job. Be it small towns or big cities, the SP found himself shuffled frequently. To his credit, he settled down with ease in a new place within weeks. Never throwing tantrums, pinpricking or highlighting paucities.

Agartala too had done its part and extended a warm welcome to the *non-Bengali* officer. Most of the staff at the West Agartala police station competed against each other to speak in Bangla-laced Hindi to make the new boss feel at home. But only managed to garner a chuckle from the amused man.

The tall, sprightly, beaming, forty-something IPS officer was admired in the government circles and everyone including the MLAs, the Governor and the CM held him in high regard for his honesty and integrity.

"Thank you, sir." The inspector nodded.

The SP smiled at the curvy and petite inspector who was as competent as any other man in the department. "You are in Homicide now, Roy?" He placed his black pen with a gold design inside the file closing it.

"Yes, sir."

"After years of solving small crimes, you are finally where the action is."

Inspector Roy gave him a half smile.

"A woman's corpse was discovered in Banamalipur. Next to the Rainbow School." The SP said without pretext. There was an unstated understanding among the cops that the news of death never needed a pretext or toning down while being conveyed. It could be delivered as-is. Without emotional frills.

Inspector Roy remained silent. SP Yadav waited for her to speak and then realising that the reticent young woman never really spoke much, continued: "This will be your first case, Roy. The corpse seems to be that of a teacher who taught at the school next door."

"When was the corpse discovered, sir?" She asked. Her face was calm. It gave away nothing.

"This morning while you were drinking tea." SP Yadav knew that she loved her cups of tea and he had deliberately mentioned it to rattle the stoic woman.

She was disconcerted by his jibe but didn't let it show. In her years of working at the police department, she had learned that wearing her emotions on her sleeve never did any good. Particularly, for a woman.

If she had expressed her fears and apprehensions in the five years of her service, she would have remained Sub Inspector in the faraway Bilonia, forever. Her first posting in the tiny town of Bilonia in South Tripura was equivalent to a punishment posting. Everyone, including her mother, had written her off. With sheer grit and hard work and by following the golden rule of *talking less and doing more*, she had made her way back to the capital of Tripura.

SP Yadav was unaware of the thoughts running at a jet set speed through the young inspector's mind. All he saw was a stubborn silence, yet again. "Get on it and report back to me. Since this is your first case in Homicide -- you will report to me bi-weekly."

"Yes, sir." The inspector saluted and turned around to leave.

"Just one more thing, Roy. SI Das will be assisting you in the investigation."

"SI Das?"

"Pritam Das from Dhaleshwar Thana. He has been transferred to Homicide as well. Rimbai didn't tell you that?" The SP chuckled.

Inspector Roy's heart sank. Her stoic mask cracked. If there was one person she never intended on meeting again, it was Pritam Das.

"He will fill you in on the case. He has been handling it since morning." The phone on the SP's large wooden desk rang like a banshee bringing the conversation to an end.

"Sure, sir." She nodded muttering under her breath. "As long as he doesn't hinder the investigation in any way."

CHAPTER V

SI Das

SI Das had this bad feeling when he woke up in the morning that something terrible was about to unfold. The recent happenings in West Tripura police station had only proven him right. First, as soon as he entered the office there was a call from constable Chakma about a couple who had discovered a corpse in their backyard.

When he asked Chakma to seal the site and call the fingerprint expert, the constable said:

"Sir, the body has begun to putrefy. What good would a fingerprint expert do?"

"Procedure, Chakma."

"But sir, the house has been vacant for a month. The couple was planning to move in a couple of days. They had been visiting the house for the past week. We will only find their fingerprints—"

"Can you leave the rest to the expert? Let them do their work. We will draw our conclusions based on the evidence." The SI cut in. Frowning he checked his WhatsApp messages. There were several texts from Puja. Ignoring the queue of texts, he read the last one.

This is not going to work. I am tired of lying to my parents. They want to meet you and your parents and fix a date for marriage. Do you even want to get married?

Grunting, the SI flung the phone on his small desk. The Xiomi phone, the only one he could afford with his meagre salary sprung to life. This time it was the SP. Without wasting a second, he answered the call.

"Sir." He said in a saluting-tone.

"Already on your first case, Das?" The SP's mocking voice echoed on the device.

"Yes, sir. We are bringing in the fingerprint expert."

"Good. I am glad to be the first one to tell you that your new boss will be Inspector Jui Roy."

"Jui Roy?" His head started to pound. Pressing his forehead, he stood with an ashen face.

"You are in good hands, Das. All the best!" The SP beamed hanging up.

SI Das stood frozen.

Jui Das? Of all the people in this god damn world!

A woman he had once loved madly but couldn't bring himself to marry. A college friend who knew him like no other. A scorned ex who had broken all ties and never seen him eye to eye.

Fucking, great!

He cried. Working under his ex-girlfriend on his first case was just what he needed to shatter his already imperfect life!

CHAPTER VI

Back to the Corpse

The upturned ground where the German Shepherd had dug and laid the corpse bare had been sealed by the police. A putrid smell pervaded the environs. A group of bystanders, which comprised of next door neighbours and locals passing through the road, next to the house stood conjecturing about the woman who had been discovered in the early hours of the winter morning from a two feet deep pit at the back of the house.

The dismayed couple sat in the living room waiting to escape from the cursed house. All they wanted now was to get away. Constable Chakma, however, held them back for further questioning. The dog who had become the hero of the ghastly episode, after wagging its tail for hours and barking at every new face was sitting next to its master. It appeared worn-out too.

The corpse lay inside a glass coffin. The teaching and non-teaching staff of Rainbow School after hearing of their ex-teacher's dreadful demise insisted that her lifeless body and what remained of it -- be carried in a coffin as a mark of respect. In less than an hour, they had managed to procure a brand new coffin and got it delivered to the deceased's address.

Jhorna, the house help sat next to the body, jittery and teary-eyed. It was she who had identified the body as that of Rituparna Bagdi, the former English teacher who had lived in the small cottage-like home for a year. The devastated woman had noticed the big silver ring in the shape of a large leaf that her employer loved wearing on all occasions. She was wearing it on her middle finger on the day she last saw her.

"It is Didi's." She had whispered crouching next to the body as constable Chakma watched closely. He noticed that the woman was shaken and not feigning shock. Each tiny detail added up to something while solving what appeared to be a clear case of homicide.

"Who is Didi?"

"Ritu di."

"Who is Ritu di?" The constable inquired calmly.

"She taught in that school." She pointed towards the tall red building that stood at the centre of a massive ground flanked by trees.

"Rainbow School?"

The maid nodded, wiping her eyes. "She gave me a sari and cake last Christmas."

"Well, this year there will be nothing." The constable shrugged.

Jhorna threw a contemptuous glance at the man's direction. The constable ignored it. He was accustomed to such looks.

The maid stood up. Fixing the pleats of her sari absentmindedly, she prepared to leave.

"You can't leave the premises," Chakma commanded noticing what the woman was up to.

"What, why? I have to go clean Gita di's house—"

"This is a murder site and you have identified the murdered victim. Hence, we will need to take your testimony." Chakma asserted robotically. He wasn't a novice handling murder cases and suspects. He had been getting his hands dirty for four years. And yet, he hadn't been promoted as the SI. But then, that was another story for another day.

"Sir, I have done nothing. I just happened to come in because Gita di next door told me that the police was here and a dog had found a dead body." Jhorna explained. Her tears had dried up magically and she had quickly recovered from the emotional turmoil that she was in, only moments ago.

"Sit down. My boss will be here any moment." Chakma hissed without paying any attention to the cries of the maid who was feeling squeamish already. The prospect of ending up in jail frightened the poor woman who had an ailing mother waiting for her in the shanty nearby.

Chakma checked the time on his watch. It was past two. The sun shone brightly warming the cold earth with its blazing rays. The police van which was supposed to take the body away to the morgue for post mortem was standing outside on the road.

"In the meantime, let me go and catch up with your Gita di." He grinned to the maid who only glared back at him.

***

Constable Chakma walked over to the two storied yellow walled house with a slanted rusty-red roof and a marron balustrade. On a road lined with blue and drab white homes, this one with a bright colour pattern stood out. Climbing the small staircase that led to the porch, he pressed the bell.

White curtains rustled inside for a moment. Before he could notice the face that had peeked, the door flung open. A short and stout woman with scrunched eyes and wrinkled forehead appeared. In a bright saffron nightie bedecked with pink wildflowers, she was an odd sight.

"Yes?" Her voice rumbled.

"Gita di?" The constable lost his smile. The peeved woman who stood in front made him fumble for words. A rarity.

"That's me. What do you want?" She crossed her short and flabby arms over her enormous bosom.

"Jhorna works in your home?"

"She must have told you that already." She scoffed. Clearly, the khaki uniform did not scare her.

"Your next door neighbour was found dead—"

"We know that but we didn't kill her. No one was here for a month." She cocked her double chin towards the house. "We were in Udaipur with my husband. You can talk to him and confirm." She said brusquely.

"Why is your husband in Udaipur?"

"To feed this family."

The constable stared at the woman in awe. Such vehement recklessness was new to him.

"He works there?"

"He is an Assistant Professor at the Udaipur College."

"What subject does he teach?"

"Political Science. Why?"

"Just as-k-king." The constable stuttered.

"Oh! I thought you were interested in getting someone admitted." She laughed.

"This is a serious interrogation." Constable Chakma said weakly.

"Of course! But, I have to cook so if you please, *sir*, may I get back to my kitchen before the fish curry is charred beyond recognition?" The insolence in the woman's voice riled the constable. He quickly turned away.

"Oh! One more thing, I almost forgot." She jeered at his back.

Chakma turned grudgingly.

"There was a stench in the air. It must have come from there." She thrust her rounded arm towards the murder site. "I had complained about it."

"Where did you complain?"

"Where would I complain? I told my neighbours about it." She rolled her small round eyes.

"Oh." Without another word, the incensed man turned around walking away.

Thankfully, there weren't any more neighbours on the other side of the house to interview. Only a narrow bylane connecting with the traffic-laden Dhaleshwar Road.

CHAPTER VII

Inspector Roy and SI Das

SI Das ambled towards the inspector's room.

A dead body awaits.

He reminded himself.

Clearing his throat he entered the small room. A large wooden desk, a new ergonomic chair – just like his, a pinboard and a whiteboard fixed beside it and a grey filing cabinet fell in his line of vision.

Inspector Roy raised her chin at the sudden arrival. His hair was tamped down. The ponytail that he sported in college and maintained painstakingly was gone. His attitude appeared to have changed too. The rebel-without-a-cause look had made way for a hardened, intrepid cop who meant business.

Paying no heed to the aggravated beating of her heart, she sprang up. His towering six feet frame reminded her yet again of her short stature and the many mean jokes she had endured from common friends, years ago.

"We can leave in the police van." She raised her head staring at him. Her face impassive.

The SI nodded. She had changed. Definitely changed. The boyish frame had transformed into the body of a woman. The pixie cut, which she sported in college to make a statement was no longer in sight. Her hair was now tied in a neat bun. Her eyes, which were earlier streaked with a poignant sadness were now tinged with feigned nonchalance.

He found his heart aflutter but chose to ignore it. "It will take us some time to reach Banamalipur. Constable Chakma called me up. The maid who was working at Rituparna Bagdi's home has been held back for questioning. The couple who had discovered the body is there too."

She nodded and without another word walked out while the SI followed. Inside the car, they remained resolutely silent. Even avoided looking at each other. When their eyes collided a few times, they turned their faces hurriedly away. The driver stared at them through the rear-view mirror wondering if a cold war had ensued between the two young cops.

After an hour, they stood in front of the body. SI Das took out his hanky pressing it closer to his nose. The rancid smell riled his insides. The body of the victim had decomposed further in the past few hours as it lay in the coffin under the shaded porch. Constable Chakma had not touched the body lest he may destroy circumstantial evidence.

The inspector stared at the body unblinkingly as if in a daze. Pensively stepping forward, she opened the coffin with a light touch of her nimble fingers.

"We will have difficulty running tests on the body. It's not in a good state." She said after a while. "Should we do an exhumation autopsy?" The SI grumbled stepping away from the corpse. He was sure that he would have trouble sleeping tonight.

She pursed her lips reflecting on the question. Her eyes fixed on the woman lying in a tattered white salwar kameez. Her upturned face was hollowed out in parts, her mouth wide open. A macabre sight and yet she didn't take her eyes off.

From childhood, Jui Roy had been fascinated by dead bodies. Some would say, enamoured by them. When her grandmother died, she wouldn't leave the dead old woman's side. Her grieving parents saw it as proof of the affectionate attachment between the two. The child did spend a lot of time with the old woman in her tiny house on the adjacent street.

Little did they know that their eight-year-old daughter was fascinated by lifeless forms and the stories that lay hidden inside their insentient bodies. Akin to a treasure chest. At home, she found a way of observing dead lizards, cockroaches and rats. When a neighbour's cat or dog succumbed to death, she ran to their homes with red and pink hibiscus flowers plucked from their bijou garden.

The neighbours welcomed her with open arms and praised the sad-eyed girl with long unruly tresses for her kindness. At school, she looked forward to the Bio class where she could sit and observe the dead specimens without having to answer questions on her atypical behaviour.

Jui Roy bent closer to the dead woman. There was a story in there. A voice muffled not by death but by a perpetrator who was still breathing under the daylight.

"Her toe and fingernails are missing." She whispered.

"Right." The SI said in a loud voice breaking the peculiar reverie that he found her in. "We might find something more in the autopsy." He added.

The inspector glowered. She didn't want to be disturbed when her thoughts were elsewhere and her mind was trying to forge a connection with the deceased.

"We don't have much to go with." The SI spoke again.

"Sir, the maid is livid. She wants to leave. She is getting late it seems." Constable Chakma said in a huff.

"Can we talk to her?" The SI said.

Inspector Roy stared at the two men in front of her. She could have done without the disruptive duo who gawked at her like she was a circus ringleader.

"All right." She muttered under her breath leading the way.

Jhorna was squatted on the living room floor. The inspector kneeled facing her. The SI stood beside his boss holding a file and a pen ready to take notes. Constable Chakma was asked to wait outside with the flustered couple who had discovered the body hours ago.

"What is your name?" The inspector asked with a calm but stern expression.

"Jhorna Das." The maid said. Her forehead still furrowed in annoyance.

"How long have you been working here?"

"I've worked for a year until Didi left a month ago."

"Where did she go?" The SI interjected.

"I don't know. I came to work at my usual time in the evening—"

"What was your usual time?" Inspector Roy asked.

The maid considered the cop for a moment. The woman was too petite to be a police officer. Only her unsmiling face and unyielding demeanour made her somewhat credible as an officer investigating the murder of a former employer.

"Around 4 p.m. I work at five homes. I do three houses in the morning. And two in the evening."

"All in this area?" The SI asked.

Jhorna nodded. "All on this road. My home is ten minutes away. I used to come to Didi's place only at 4-4.30 p.m. She taught in that school." She flailed her thin arms girdled by bright gold imitation bangles at the direction of the school.

"When did you usually leave?"

"At around 5.30 p.m. Sometimes earlier. There was never much to do. Didi never made me work too hard." Jhorna smiled longingly for the departed soul.

"When was the last time you saw her?" The inspector lowered her voice. She didn't want to come across as inconsiderate to the maid. In her years of investigation, Jui Roy had learned that a show of concern and gentleness often led to a useful flow of information.

The maid thought for a while. She raised her chin to look at the only man in the room.

"Can you give us a moment alone?" The inspector said slowly – her gaze fixed at Jhorna.

"Okay." The SI stomped out of the room vexed by her instruction. He didn't like it one bit that his ex-girlfriend was now dictating matters at work. Swallowing his pride, he stood next to the constable. "Got a Gold flake?"

Chakma held the white and beige stick in front of his boss who appeared ruffled.

"Tell me." Inspector Roy smiled faintly once the SI had departed. "If you want, you can take a look at your mobile and tell me the time and day."

The maid removed the sari from her bony chest exposing her jutting collar bone. Sinking her hands deeper into her skinny bosom, she took her purse out – a tatty plastic pouch with a faded Donald Duck design. Opening the zip with unsteady fingers, she cleared her throat.

The inspector waited patiently. Making no attempt at conversation. The art of conversation had left her befuddled and uncomfortable, her entire life. However, this very weakness had turned into an advantage at her workplace. Silence, she discovered was a potent weapon deadlier than artful chatter.

"Here," Jhorna said at last thrusting the phone at the inspector.

Inspector Roy ran her eyes over the list of numbers on her jet black Nokia phone, purchased recently. It took her a while to focus on the array of numbers on display. The *unsmart* Nokia phone needed time and patience.

The inspector squinted her eyes in attention. "She called you on 21 November, why?" The Inspector raised her eyes, fixing it on the maid.

Jhorna shifted in her chair. She didn't like the way the woman was staring at her. The fact that her former employer was lying with her bone and flesh exposed right outside the house made her shudder.

"This is a routine investigation, Jhorna. No one is accusing you of anything." The inspector assured.

"Didi called me at noon and asked if I could come at 6. She..." The maid's voice trailed off.

The inspector sat silently.

"She said that she would be coming home late from school."

"Did she tell you why?"

"No." Jhorna opened her mouth to speak but stopped herself.

"You did have a hunch though."

Jhorna stared at her wide-eyed. She didn't know that the woman was a mind reader too. "I-I am not sure, madam. It was just a guess."

"What was your guess?"

"I think she was with someone and she didn't want to be disturbed."

"And you thought that someone was—"

"Her husband," Jhorna murmured.

"Her husband?"

"Yes, Mrinal Da. He used to visit her sometimes."

"So Rituparna was married?"

"No, she was divorced." The maid corrected her.

"So he was her ex-husband?"

Jhorna nodded.

"Why did he come visiting if they were estranged?"

"Dada loved Didi. I could see the way he looked at her. But, I don't know if Didi loved him." Jhorna wasn't frightened of speaking her mind anymore. She felt quite comfortable talking to the sensitive and intuitive cop.

"Did they fight or argue when they met?" The inspector knew that married couples invariably bickered, particularly divorced couples.

"No." She said thinking hard. "They never argued. They spoke very little in front of me. "

"Did you notice anything unusual on 21 November? The day you saw her last."

Jhorna reflected for a moment. "She was silent and jumpy. Usually, Didi talks when I go around doing my chores. But that day she was just...silent."

"How long were you here?"

Jhorna looked around the near empty living room dispiritedly. "Maybe an hour—"

"So when you left -- it was 7PM?"

"Maybe, I can't be sure."

"Last question." The inspector said in a considerate tone. She didn't want to hold back the poor woman any longer whose source of livelihood depended on the goodwill of her employers in whose homes she worked all day. "What made you think that there was someone else with her when she called and asked you to come later?"

"I don't remember." Jhorna conceded. "It has been more than a month. Also, I am not sure if Didi was with someone.

It's a...guess."

"If you remember anything, do give me a call. Here's my number." Inspector Roy slowly dictated the digits of her phone number, while Jhorna pressed her device innumerable times diligently, saving the number under the name *Police Didi*.

When she was done, the inspector asked, "Can you give me your Didi's number?"

Jhorna dictated the digits slowly and waited for the inspector to save the number. She was somewhat disappointed when the inspector saved it as RB.

Just RB.

CHAPTER VIII

The Honeymooning Couple

SI Das approached the couple who were huddled together at one end of the porch. Their dog, Kuttush sat next to them. When the large creature saw the approaching cops, it barked in anticipation. Although its bark sounded more like a weary growl.

Inspector Roy didn't mind the dog. Domesticated pets didn't frighten her. However, she wouldn't go so far as calling herself a dog lover. SI Das ignored the dog and promptly walked over to the couple. The inspector stopped at a distance from the SI. When he turned, she gave him a slight nod -- a cue for him to proceed with the questioning alone.

"What are your names and how long have you been waiting here?" The SI addressed the calm and diminutive husband.

The wife answered. "His name is Bimal Dutta and I'm his wife Amrita Dutta. We've been here for hours. We did nothing. If only we knew..." She glanced at the inspector whose stoic demeanour discouraged her from rattling further. She felt silent abruptly.

"We've been waiting here since Kuttush discovered the body." The husband said.

"Did you know Rituparna Bagdi?" The SI stepped closer to the couple.

"No. We didn't even know her name until the constable told us. The landlord never told us about the former tenant and we never asked." Bimal explained. Talking made him tired. He took a moment to catch his breath. His dog snuggled closer to his master. He patted him lovingly running his small tawny fingers over its thick brown mane.

"Who was she?" The wife asked.

"She was a teacher at the Rainbow School." The SI replied.

"Why would someone kill her?"

"That is what we are trying to find out." Inspector Roy cut in. "Tell me who owns this house?"

"Sunil Lahiri. He lives in Krishnanagar. Owns many homes. This is one of his homes." Amrita wanted to speak more but her husband intervened. "We didn't know that this would happen. We came here to start a new life. Although now, we will have to be cautious while looking for homes—"

"Who knows what you will find in them!" The SI jeered.

The inspector observed the couple. They didn't seem to take offence. If at all, they shared the same sentiment. Stepping closer she stood next to the SI. "What was the first thing you noticed when Kuttush dragged the body out?"

"There was no blood." Amrita blurted.

"How could there be any? It has been lying beneath the soil for some time."

"For how long?" Bimal whispered.

"For a month at the least." The inspector said. The SI glared. He should have been informed first of the findings.

"To me, it appears like she was uninjured before she was buried," Bimal murmured pensively.

"What makes you say that?"

"I've seen dead bodies. My brother died in a bike accident. His body was crushed by a lorry. We could barely recognise him." He patted his dog again. His eyes were fixed on the black granite floor of the porch. The sun had begun to set painting the world with a dash of bright colours.

The cops waited. SI Das cast a quick glance at his boss.

"Her body looks unscathed. Even if someone did kill her, it doesn't look like they used force." Bimal said eventually.

The inspector addressed her subordinate. "Take their numbers. If needed, they will have to come down to the Thana. Seal the house. We will need to talk to Sunil Lahiri as soon as possible. And take the body to the morgue."

The SI nodded. "Are we getting an exhumation autopsy done?"

"We will talk about that later." The inspector ambled away from the site of murder.

Once the cops left in the police van, Amrita asked her husband, "What made you say that?"

"Say what?"

"That she was not harmed in any way."

"Of course, she was harmed. She was murdered. All I said was that it didn't look like she was hurt before she was killed. Come, we will head home. It's late."

"Where will we live now?" Amrita rolled her eyes in exasperation.

"We will live with my parents until we find a new place," Bimal said caressing Kuttush, the dog he had named after Tintin's nifty pet dog. In his boyhood, he had read extensively about the adventures of the journo-sleuth with spiky hair, created masterfully by Herge. Albeit, in Bangla, owing to his Bangla-medium education.

And in Bangla, Snowy, the Wire Fox Terrier and Tintin's perfect companion was named Kuttush.

CHAPTER IX

Sunil Lahiri

"How am I to know that the woman was buried?" Sunil Lahiri yelled. His tall, brawny frame and large bleary eyes, which overshadowed the rest of his face, each time he opened his mouth didn't deter Inspector Roy from asserting:

"She was killed and buried in your property. Logically, you are our first suspect."

"I will get my lawyer—"

"No lawyer in the world will be able to change the indubitable fact that you were hiding a corpse in your backyard." SI Das levelled.

Lahiri opened his mouth to yell. But, decided to hold himself back. It took him some effort to do that. "I wasn't hiding anyone." He snarled scratching his chin.

"When did Rituparna Bagdi vacate your home?" The inspector said in an even tone. Although she didn't like the man, she did everything in her power to hide it.

Sunil Lahiri ran his long, thick fingers through his hair. He stank of alcohol and *gutka*. The three were sitting in a musty interrogation room, which was cleaned with phenyl in the morning but still carried a hint of vomit and urine.

"She never told me anything. I wasn't informed. I had to call the principal of her school, Father Joseph. He told me that she had resigned over mail and left town. How was I to know that someone had bumped her off?"

"Did you bump her off?" The inspector said in an incisive tone. At times, volatile suspects only needed a trigger to spill the beans and ended up giving vital clues.

Sunil Lahiri considered the short, curvy woman with deep, sad eyes. He never liked speaking to women. They had their use – in bed and the kitchen. Other than that he didn't like having them around. His wife, a prosaic nag was useless in bed too.

When he woke up this morning, he had no clue that during the course of the day, he would be interrogated by a female inspector and asked incendiary questions. It raked his nerves and made him dour.

He drawled indulgently. "I...did...not...kill...her."

The inspector changed tactic. She knew the man didn't like a khaki-clad woman. "Then you have nothing to be afraid of." She said in a mollifying tone.

"Unless of course, you are hiding something." The SI swallowed a laugh.

"I'm not going to rent my homes to outsiders from now on. They come and go and I get interrogated by the police."

"Outsiders?" Inspector Roy raised her chin.

"That woman was from Kolkata. She was not from here. These women...who knows what they do! They say that they are here to teach but..." Lahiri left his statement hanging staring hard at the inspector.

Inspector Roy understood what he was insinuating but she refused to react. With experience, she had learned to distance herself from sexists and misogynists. In the hands of a manipulator, those were potent weapons to rattle and divert an unsuspecting soul. And Jui Roy was not new to the game of subterfuge.

"Do you want us to resort to third degree?" The SI sprang up from the chair. The *gutka*-chewing asshole was getting on his nerves.

Lahiri stared insolently at the tall and lean man inviting him to lose his temper.

The SI granted his wish. Without another word, he punched the smug man. Crimson red spittle blasted from his mouth in full force due to the impact of the sudden punch. Lahiri rubbed his wide palms over his mouth and cheeks in shock.

The inspector stared at the men in astonishment. The sound of the SI's undulating breaths and Lahiri's blood smeared face made the Inspector hiss:

"I want you to share everything that you know about the deceased, or things will get much worse."

Lahiri's head reeled. He hadn't eaten since morning and last night he had too much to drink. He wanted to bash the bastard who stood before him like he owned this shithole. But, he let it slide. In his years of running a business, he knew better.

Inspector Roy shifted in her chair. "Tell me something, when Rituparna vanished overnight, what happened to her things?"

Lahiri stopped rubbing his chin, which still hurt. Just like the cops, he wanted this interrogation to end. Forcibly lowering his voice he addressed the inspector, "I've kept her things locked in one of my storerooms. I did find it strange that she didn't bother to collect her things. And..." His voice broke as he felt parched. "Can I get water?" He croaked.

"Do we look like waiters?" SI Das hissed. "Spit it out, Lahiri."

Inspector Roy observed the man for a moment. Silently, she stood up and walked out while the SI shrugged. He knew that she had gone to fetch water.

She returned holding a dirty white plastic jug and a steel glass. She poured a glass handing it over to Lahiri. When he had guzzled two glasses of water, he said, "She had left her diary. I found it hidden among her things—"

"What do you mean?" The Inspector lost her stoic calm for the first time. A faint pattern began to form in front of her eyes.

"Her diary was hidden under layers of clothing in her steel almirah. She had purchased a new almirah. Of course, my house is furnished with chairs, a bed and a small table. But, if the tenant wishes to buy—"

"We are not looking to rent your apartment anytime soon." SI Das scoffed.

"Did you have fun reading her journal?" Inspector Roy murmured holding the man's gaze.

"I didn't touch that book. I won't violate someone's privacy. Plus, I don't have the time to read diaries."

"Coming from you it does seem unlikely." The SI scoffed.

"When did you call Father Joseph? We need the exact date and time." She said after a pause.

Lahiri took his mobiles out. Both, Apple smartphones of the latest make and model. Without a thought, he browsed through the call list on one of his phones. "Here. I called him on 25 November. She wasn't picking my calls." He said raising his gaze.

Inspector Roy scanned the call list. "Why did you call her? It wasn't the first of the month so couldn't have been for rent."

"I wanted to know if she will be renewing the rental contract. I didn't know if she planned on staying for another year."

"You maintain rental contracts!" The SI taunted.

"I run a legitimate business." He said defensively.

The SI laughed. The inspector didn't. "Do you renew your contracts annually?"

"I do. I was supposed to increase the rent as well."

"How much was she paying?"

"Nine thousand. I had asked for ten but she requested that I lessen the rent so I did."

"You are a kind man, aren't you?" SI Das smiled disdainfully.

"I try--"

"What is the nature of your business?" The inspector interrupted leaning forward.

"I rent out houses and run a travel agency. I make air bookings for national and international travel." He retorted with a phony composure.

"Where is this agency?"

"It's in Battala."

The inspector rose from the chair. "We will need to look at the deceased's belongings. I hope you are aware that you can't leave town until we close this case." Before the stunned Lahiri could utter a word, she walked out of the room.

SI Das followed chuckling to himself. It had been a while since he had punched a man in the interrogation room.

"Before he leaves, get Father Joseph's number. We will have to talk to him. And we will go to Lahiri's place and recover Rituparna's things. Hopefully, her diary has not been tampered with." She walked over to her desk.

"Do we need the fingerprint expert?"

"We have lost all fingerprints for sure. It has been a month. Sunil Lahiri touched her stuff and god knows, who! Still, we need to follow protocol."

"Should we get a cup of tea before proceeding to Lahiri's home?" The SI said hesitantly while his phone blared.

He took his phone out. The number that flashed on the screen made him curse under his breath. He cut the call instantly.

"Who is that?" She was amused by his sudden change of manner.

"No one. Personal." He mumbled. "Tea?"

She nodded.

CHAPTER X

Rituparna's Diary

January, 2018

Agartala is just like any other small Indian town. Complacent. Proud. And unexposed. I don't mind it much. I spend most of my waking hours in school among my students. They occupy my time and thoughts.

It has been a month in my new role as the English teacher at the Rainbow School. I've been teaching prose, verse and grammar to the middle and high school students.

Before joining, I was apprehensive about my students. I had wondered if they were any different from the way we were a decade or so ago. I am not much older than them – my youngest students are fifteen years apart in time. It wasn't the age gap that concerned me but the time these children spent on internet-fuelled devices. They seem to have more information and data points to converse on. Their faces were strained with overexposure to information, which had no bearing upon their childhoods.

On my first day at Rainbow School, when I walked into the large, spacious well-lit classrooms and cast a sweeping glance at their eager, uncertain and half-afraid faces, strangely, my fear and apprehensions vanished. Just like that, I was transported to my school days.

As I spent more and more time with them, I came to realise that despite technological leaps, deep inside, they were still child-like. Excitable. Sensitive. And in need of love, affection and appreciation.

I made it a point to not only impart knowledge, which was my primary KRA but I also gave them my wa rmest smile and words of encouragement. To find their faces light up when I walked into class; to hear them shout, "Rituparna Ma'am will take this period, yay," made my heart sing.

Last week, I was asked to fill in for the senior Maths teacher, Jha Sir in the twelfth grade. He had been held up by the principal for an academic review. I had just finished my lunch with Dipti, who teaches Social Science to the middle school students.

Dipti loves to cook and her lunch boxes are filled with scrumptious vegetarian delicacies prepared with care. She brings in a new dish each day. Usually, I carry sandwiches for lunch. Dipti views it as the bane of being single and unattached.

"That's why you must get married. You get a home, which comes with a kitchen and a husband."

"I thought you would put the husband before your well-stuffed kitchen." I laughed.

She laughed too in her careless, loud fashion as her voluptuous frame jiggled in mirth.

Once I had wrapped up lunch, I walked over to the classroom, which is located at the end of the first floor. I had no trouble finding the class as I teach them English. From the corridor, I could hear a loud din. Increasing my pace I entered the classroom hastily before Father Joseph could dart in with an accusatory look on his face. The principal of the Rainbow School is a strict man who values discipline over everything else.

When the students saw me, they fell silent abruptly. There was just one boy who kept his legs crossed on his desk. He does that in every class. His name is Paul Jamatia.

Ignoring Paul's act of defiance, which did rattle me a little, I started flipping through the Mathematics textbook.

"Which chapter are you on?" I asked a girl with glasses who was seated at the front.

"Calculus. Chapter 5, ma'am." The girl answered timidly.

"Did you just start--"

"We have just started, ma'am. Maybe you can help us with understanding differential calculus better. We do have some doubts." Paul yelled from the last bench.

"I will if you help me understand why your legs are resting on the desk." I smiled at him.

He stared at me for a moment before removing his feet off the desk. "Now, your turn. Explain."

Without paying any heed to his words which did sound like a challenge, I began at the very beginning. With the illustrious ones who invented this branch of mathematical analysis, the renowned English physicist and scientist Isaac Newton and Leibniz, the German philosopher and mathematician and continued to explain how differential calculus was more than non-constant rates of change and functions. Further, I explained how understanding calculus was vital to mathematical programming and other branches of science and even business.

At the end of the session when I walked out, the class had fallen silent. Only hushed whispers could be heard.

Although it was a different experience, I had forgotten all about it and got busy with teaching language and literature. Two days later, when Jha Sir stormed in during lunch and stood gasping before us, I wondered if anything was the matter.

Dipti wasn't happy about the sudden intrusion. She had just opened her box of red carrot halwa garnished with nuts, raisins and cherries. An inviting aroma emanated from her box.

"Did you teach calculus in my class?" Jha Sir glowered at me.

"Father Joseph asked me to fill in—"

He didn't let me finish. "Exactly, he asked you to fill in. Not teach."

"The students had doubts. I tried clarifying—"

"And you think you are qualified to clear their doubts."

"Did something happen?" I asked instead.

"Paul Jamatia wrote on the blackboard that Ritu Ma'am must teach us Mathematics. Not Jha!"

Dipti giggled. I tried controlling my laughter but snorted.

"I am sorry. That wasn't my intention—"

"I don't care about your intention. You are not qualified to teach Mathematics. I have done a Ph.D. on the subject. You are just an English teacher. Go, teach Shakespeare or something—"

"I don't have a doctorate in Maths—"

"Exactly, my point." He snapped.

"But, I do have a Masters so I know what I am doing." I smiled. "Moreover, I know the quality of Ph.D. degree holders in and around me. No offence, but a doctorate degree doesn't guarantee that you are an authority on the subject. In my experience, it's often the opposite. Sir, learning isn't about garnering degrees."

"I will talk to Father Joseph about it." He threatened.

"Please do. Should we go now? I'm done with my lunch." I piped up closing my lunch box.

"I haven't eaten." He grumbled storming off as Dipti and I broke into peals of laughter.

CHAPTER XI

Rituparna's Baggage

Inspector Roy closed the diary and slowly put it aside. She was wearing gloves but she knew that she didn't have to bother with destroying evidence. The evidence had already been ruined. Forty one days elapsed after the crime was committed and the body was discovered.

"Did you find anything important?" She asked SI Das who had been rummaging through all the suitcases for the past few hours. They were sitting in the tiny storeroom at the back of Sunil Lahiri's bungalow at Krishnanagar.

"I don't think any of her clothes, books and cutlery can be counted as important evidence. She does have an impressive collection of books and several saris in the same colour and pattern." He murmured more to himself.

"Those blue saris are worn by female teachers of the Rainbow School."

"That's their uniform, you mean." He remarked.

The inspector nodded. "Her diary can be counted as an important piece of evidence. I will have to read all her entries. I couldn't manage to read more than a few."

The SI considered his boss whom he knew a bit too well. "You think that's enough evidence to crack the case?"

"It will help us to get started and connect the dots. Plus, we have her passport, Adhar card, school badge and a few bags. You may find a laptop in there."

"We don't have her phone, yet." He ran his eyes over the many things spattered on the floor.

She reflected for a moment. "The question is why? Why is her phone missing?

"The culprit might have taken it away. Could it be Lahiri?"

"Could be. But, we can't force him to hand it over—"

"Why not?"

"By now, he must have obtained a lawyer to protect himself. And got rid of the phone." She said with a faraway look in her eyes.

The SI continued to look through Rituparna's things. "Here. Take a look at this." He held a white photo frame in his outstretched hands.

Running her fingers over the picture, she looked at it intently. "Her parents...and her."

"Are you sure?" The SI considered the picture too.

"Why else would she frame it and keep it with her?"

"She must be what four or five?" He kept his eyes on the photo frame. Although her sudden proximity did disrupt his breathing rhythm. Exhaling deeply, he tried focussing on the photo and the job in hand.

A young girl in a red frock stood clutching the arms of her tall father and a relatively short mother, smiling faintly. The father in black rimmed glasses stared with a neutral expression. His lips making no effort to smile. It was the mother who draped in a moss green silk sari with red borders grinned making up for the lack of joy in the family.

Inspector Roy rose from the creaky wooden chair she had been sitting on. "I will head back to Rainbow School and talk to the principal and Dipti." She held the frame at the SI.

He took it. "Who is Dipti?"

"Rituparna's colleague." She walked towards the door.

"I checked up on Mrinal Chatterjee. The ex-husband of Rituparna." He yelled at her disappearing frame.

She turned around.

"He is not in town. Lives in Kolkata. Shobha Bazaar. We called and informed him about his ex-wife—"

"How did you track him?" She interjected.

"Constable Chakma found his contact number from the maid, Jhorna."

She thought for a moment before asking, "How did he react?"

"He broke down weeping. He will be landing in Agartala tonight. He has promised to help us with the investigation."

"And you think that's proof of his innocence."

"He didn't fake the act."

"Are you sure? Mrinal Chatterjee is a professional actor. He is all over social media." The inspector flinched. She had checked the actor's Facebook, Instagram and Twitter pages. Her quick research on the actor had left her feeling confounded. She couldn't fathom why everyone wanted to post pictures of themselves and divulge what they felt randomly.

For years now, as part of ongoing investigations, checking social media profiles had become mandatory. Not that it didn't lead to discrepancies. A person's social media profile or the projected image could be starkly different from the real person.

"Is Rituparna on social media?" The SI kicked another suitcase away stepping closer.

"No."

"An introvert." He said in a knowing tone, which reminded her of a shared past and mindless teasing and banter. A past that seemed so distant now that it didn't even feel real anymore.

"I know what you mean." She held his gaze.

He smiled saying nothing.

"She and I are similar that way. We are not on Facebook, Instagram or Twitter. An aberration." The inspector muttered under her breath walking away.

45

CHAPTER XII

Jhorna

Jhorna lay on the cane mat, her glazed eyes fixed on the tin roof. Crows cawed blatantly nearby. These days the crows cawed all day. Even at nights. Their shrill voice overpowering every sound and smell in their tiny shanty. Her old, ailing mother who had shrivelled to half her size due to Cancer winced and turned on the shoddy wooden bed.

Maa's pain had her worried in the beginning. With time it became a nibbling constant that she couldn't get rid of. Most of what she earned by working at five homes was spent on medicines. The doctors had given Maa six months but she had been in this condition for more than a year now.

Sometimes, she wondered if Maa's absence would come to affect her the way she often envisioned. On some days, she was certain that her affectionate mother who had never raised her voice even once since her birth would be in a better place -- if she died. This world wasn't for poor people.

It didn't seem like it belonged to the educated and the rich either. Death did strike everyone with its shiny, sharp axe. Why else would Didi die so suddenly? She was almost her age. Maybe a few years older.

Her heart thudded each time she thought about the woman who had only months ago smiled at her and given her leftover food and her not-so-old nighties. She still wore those cotton nighties that were a size larger for her bony frame.

Do I tell the constable about that evening? Will he understand?

She thought aloud. Hearing her voice which she had never liked made her unsure and eroded her determination. She had wanted to confide in that woman inspector with unusually steady eyes but couldn't.

What would she think of me if she knew that I had seenhim loitering in the house that evening, a day after Didi went missing?

Didi wasn't the kind to disappear overnight. She was brave. Why else would she leave her folks in Kolkata and work in an unknown place among strangers?

The police won't understand. They will hold me back for further interrogation if they realised that I had seen the murderer.

I will have to do rounds of the Thana and court.

And I know how that turns out for poor people. It destroys their life and peace.

With a resolute look on her face, she leaped up from the mat turning the single-burner gas stove on. Rummaging through the large plastic basket, she found a bunch of long tender bamboo shoots chopped and wrapped in an old newspaper. Dropping the shoots in a mud bowl, she opened the large steel jar filled to its brim with dried fish. Jhorna made sure that the steel jar was never bereft of *shidol* fish, a family favourite.

"I will make a neat bamboo *godok* for dinner, Maa," She yelled smiling unwaveringly at her mother who only grunted in response.

Moments later, when Jhorna sat at Maa's bedside feeding her, she had made up her mind. She was not going to tell the police about that evening. Or, about the man she had watched surreptitiously, hiding behind the unlit lamp post.

CHAPTER XIII

Father Joseph

The long bearded principal, with salt and pepper hair and whose teeth was as white as the chalks that rested on his table, stood up extending his hand towards Inspector Roy, as soon as she walked into his room. She shook them warmly. The man had a solemn countenance, which was needed in a job that called for asserting a degree of authority often.

"My condolences to Ms Bagdi's family. I hope that her mother has recuperated. Although I have no words to console her. There is no greater sorrow than the pain of losing one's child."

"Rituparna lost her parents when she was a child. She was raised by her aunt. I will pass on your message to her, when we meet."

"Oh, yes, yes! Pardon my lapse of memory." Father Joseph failed to hide his surprise at hearing the news. Although he did try hard.

The inspector pulled a chair to sit. "Thank you for making the time, Father."

"It is my duty as a responsible citizen of the civic society to help the police. I want to see the culprit caught and put behind bars."

She smiled wanly. "What kind of teacher was Rituparna Bagdi?"

The principal paused arranging his thoughts. He knew if he spoke too much, he could run into trouble with the police. Being cordial and cooperative was one thing but ending up at the police station to testify meant missing hours at work. He couldn't afford to do that.

Father Joseph was incapable of delegating work or trusting someone to carry out the job.

"She was a competent and dedicated teacher just like her skilled counterparts." He declared.

The inspector noticed the delay in his response.

"What subjects did she teach?" She perused casually.

"English to middle and senior school students."

"I was under the impression that she taught Mathematics as well to the senior students."

Father Joseph Thomas blinked. "What gave you that impression—"

"She did have a Master's degree in Mathematics. Didn't you check her credentials when she joined?"

"You can be sure of that. We have a stringent and systematic practice in place wherein we thoroughly check the credentials of all our staff. We also have a rigorous and meticulous background verification process."

"And yet, you had no clue that your English teacher was moonlighting as a Mathematics tutor."

She waited for the import of her words to hit the self-assured man who quite clearly didn't like the police. Although he claimed otherwise.

"I had no idea that she was giving tuitions." The principal said softly.

"Many of your teachers do. Virendra Jha, for example, does."

He considered the woman sitting in front of him. She was sharp but precocious. And he didn't like what she was implying. "You see inspector, what the teachers do outside the school premises or in their free time is not my concern. I've enough on my plate already." He smiled high-handedly.

"Sure, Father. You don't mind if I talk to your teachers."

"Of course. Please do what you need to do."

"Before I talk to them, I would like to see the resignation mail that Rituparna Bagdi sent."

"Sure. Let me dig that out for you." The Father smiled openly this time. More out of relief than anything else.

After looking through his inbox for a few minutes, he pulled out Rituparna's last mail. Flipping his grey sleek laptop towards the cop, he blurted in joy, "Here. This is the mail."

Dear Sir,

I regret to inform you that I am leaving town tomorrow. My aunt, I am afraid, is severely ill and she wants me by her side. I did try to reason with her about finishing the term at least. But, she is adamant.

She says I can finish the term and see her in three months' time. Although she doesn't know if it will be her insentient body or her breathing form I will encounter. She had called from the hospital to unfold this piece of drama upon me.

Aunts, just like mothers are strange. They have their way of wielding emotion to get what they want.

I apologize for the trouble that my sudden departure will cause. I hope another teacher will fill in at the earliest.

Best wishes.

Yours Sincerely,

Rituparna

The Inspector noted the time and date. It was sent on 22 November at 2.30 a.m. An odd time to mail one's employer.

"Did she come to school on 22 November?" The inspector said thoughtfully staring at the calendar on top of the principal's desk.

Father followed the inspector's gaze. "No, she was absent on that day. It was a Thursday. It did catch me by surprise that she never mentioned it on the day we met for a minute—"

"Why did you meet?"

"We wanted to discuss the upcoming Sports Meet. Since she was popular with the kids and had handled the Annual Day ably, I wanted her to coordinate this event too."

"Was she nervous that day?" The inspector forwarded the email to her account returning the laptop to the principal.

"I didn't notice anything unusual if that's what you mean--"

"Apart from the faculty, I would like to meet a few students." She cut in.

The principal pursed his lips in disapproval. Akin to what he did when he stood facing a class of unruly students.

"Your uniform inspector," He cleared his throat. "It will startle the teachers as well as the students. My poor children are innocent. They are already saddened by the demise of their beloved teacher."

"I will come back tomorrow dressed in civilian clothes." Inspector Roy picked up her khaki cap from the desk. "I've no intention of scaring anyone. We are but doing our duty."

"Of course, ma'am. I understand that more than anyone else. My elder brother is in the army. He is a Major."

The mention of family made the inspector murmur thoughtfully, "Do you have any pictures of her? She wasn't on social media and we have no point of reference—"

The principal was disappointed at her lack of regard for his illustrious brother, but he hid it well. Standing up he beamed rather uncharacteristically, "Sure. Let me see if I can find something."

He began searching the steel shelves filled with several files and folders. Minutes later, he took out a picture from a thick brown file. "Here. This is what we have on file."

The inspector looked at the grim young woman who stared back at her. On that heart shaped face, apart from a hooked nose, what stood out were those deep black eyes and their penetrating gaze. For a moment, Inspector Roy felt like she was staring at Rituparna Bagdi and not her passport size picture.

"I will keep this. Thanks." The inspector stood up. "I will be back tomorrow in child-friendly clothes." She declared robotically walking out.

Once the inspector was out of the school premises, the principal called his assistant, Pintso Bhutia to his room. "I want you to call SP Yadav."

"Now, sir?" The lanky chap asked promptly.

"No, tomorrow!"

"Okay, sir," Pintso answered deferentially.

"Jesus! Remind me again, why did I hire you?" Father Joseph grumbled.

"My father died of a heart attack. You let me have his job. As the only bread earner of the family, you have my gratitude."

CHAPTER XIV

The Aunt

SI Das scratched his chin impatiently in front of the old woman. His skin had been itchy since morning. Even his throat was parched. He didn't want to believe that the call he had received earlier in the day had anything to do with his discomfort.

At around eight while he was hastily getting ready for the office, his phone rang. Assured that it was someone from the office, he picked it up without noticing the number. As luck would have it, before he could even say *hello*, she cried in her child-like voice, "My parents have agreed to meet you. This Sunday, baby. I am so excited. I can't wait for them to see you. Do you think that you should come dressed up as a cop, you look so sexy—"

"Puja, Puja. Hold on." His voice, crabby and irascible. "What do you mean? I don't understand."

"Don't you want to meet my Mom and Dad, baby?" She cooed.

He breathed sharply a couple of times. Whoever said breathing in and out was a good way to calm oneself down was surely bluffing. "We have known each other for...a month—"

"Forty-six days, baby. But, it does feel like we are made for each other. Doesn't it?"

"Puja, I am getting late for office." He said in a low voice.

"Are you coming or not?" She insisted.

He hated to do this on the phone but she was leaving him with no other option. For the past few weeks, she had been calling him incessantly. At work. At home. When he dodged her calls, she resorted to texting him. Non-stop.

"I can't meet your parents." He said slowly.

"Why not?"

"I am not ready."

"What? I thought we had connected."

He clicked his tongue. "Look, I have to go. My boss is calling. I will call, I mean I will text you. Okay?"

She didn't respond.

"Puja? Are you there?"

He could hear her sobbing.

"P-u-j-a."

"You don't love me. You have never loved me—"

"It has only been a month—"

"Forty six days, damn it!" She squealed cutting the call.

When he reached the office an hour later, he found a shrivelled old woman sitting at his desk. Constable Chakma came in running when he saw his boss walk in like he had been bitten by a sick dog.

"Good morning, sir." He grinned. "Everything all right?"

The SI glared.

Clearing his throat, Chakma whispered, "A Kanta Bagdi is here, sir."

"Why are you whispering?" The SI shrugged.

"She can hear us." He pointed his chin towards the old woman.

"When did she arrive?"

"She arrived an hour ago. She is not a talker, sir." Chakma whispered casting a furtive glance at the woman.

"Where is the inspector?"

"She is at her desk, already."

"It's only 8:45. I am never late. I had to attend an important call—"

"Sure, sir." Chakma smiled awkwardly. "I will call the inspector."

***

The cops stood facing the old woman, draped in a plain off-white sari with a black border. Her face was downcast and her eyes were dry and dead. As if someone had squashed her spirit eons ago.

"You can take all her belongings and paraphernalia. We will not hold back anything that belonged to Rituparna—"

"Where is she?" The woman raised her eyes for the first time since her arrival.

"Her body has been taken away for post-mortem. We will get it back and hand it over to you at the earliest." The SI said.

The woman didn't look at him. She kept her eyes fixed on the inspector. "Why did they kill her?" She said tersely.

"We will find out who killed Rituparna. I assure you of that." The inspector promised.

The old woman held the inspector's gaze. "Ritu and I never spoke much. She called me when she could. Not too often. Sometimes after three, sometimes after four...months." Her thin wilted lips quivered. Clutching the end of her sari she took a moment to articulate the thoughts and images that were running wildly through her mind.

"Does Mrinal know?" Mrs Bagdi asked after a while.

"We have informed him." The SI declared.

"What did he say?" She addressed the inspector.

"We will be speaking to him soon. At this point, we don't know much about him. We will find out though." Inspector Roy didn't want to reveal that Mrinal Chatterjee had broken down on the phone when SI Das informed about his ex-wife's demise. Or that he had reached Agartala a day ago.

55

"Where was he at the time of her death?" Mrs Bagdi rasped surprising them.

"He was in Agartala." The inspector confided.

The old woman scrunched her eyes. "That alcoholic. She should have never married that pitiful excuse of a human being. A girl like her. A prodigy."

The inspector waited silently. She knew the woman had more to share.

Encouraged by her silence, Mrs Bagdi went on. "He hails from a rich family. But, of what use is money if one can't keep it? Spends it all on his liquor and hobby. Actor! Never became one. Never had it in him. My poor girl. She trusted him but what did he do to her..." Her voice trailed off.

"What did he do?" The SI asked lowering his voice. He understood the delicacy of the situation but couldn't help himself from using it as an opportunity to dig deeper.

Mrs Bagdi ignored him once again.

"Make sure that he is hanged." There was a tightness around her wrinkled mouth.

"We can't confirm if Mrinal Chatterjee is the killer." The inspector said in a distant tone. She didn't like pre-mature deductions based on unfounded and prejudiced notions.

"Who else will want to kill her? She was a teacher who taught students. Teachers don't get murdered—"

"She wasn't only a teacher." The SI retorted.

Mrs Bagdi looked him in the eye. "She was a young woman living alone. An unconventional and popular teacher who could teach two subjects."

SI Das felt cornered. "I didn't mean to--"

"She was a gifted child. At school, she could crack college level mathematical sums. Her classmates were jealous of her. People were always envious of her. Even when she married that nincompoop Mrinal, they thought she had bagged a handsome, rich man." The grieving woman paused to catch her breath.

"What about Rituparna's parents?" The inspector asked softly.

Mrs Bagdi raised her gaze slowly. "They died in an accident when she was a child. They had left her with me and gone to watch a late night show..." She wringed her hands to stop herself from weeping aloud. "I have come to take her with me. I don't want to spend a day more in this cursed place. I had advised her to never leave Kolkata but then, she was always stubborn."

"We will get the autopsy report in a few weeks. Until that time, it's advisable that you stay in a hotel." The SI tilted his head towards his boss.

Inspector Roy nodded. "Mrs Bagdi, if I may ask...where is your husband?"

"Somewhere in Bihar. He works there as a doctor tending to villagers. We separated several years ago."

"May I know why?"

"He wanted me to accompany him and I didn't want to leave Kolkata." She said without a trace of emotion.

"Oh." The inspector shifted her gaze towards the SI.

The SI shook his head. He had no further questions.

None of them mentioned the diary.

I will hand it over to her after the case is closed.

The inspector promised inaudibly.

Slowly ironing the pleats of her sari with her craggy arms, the aunt stood up. Without sparing a glance at the cops, she dragged the old grey suitcase dawdling out of the room.

CHAPTER XV

SP Yadav

Inspector Roy sat opposite her boss staring at the picture frame facing the door. The smiling Yadav family reminded her of the family photos that her mother loved looking at -- every Sunday. Those old pictures always made her mother smile longingly at a past which was complete and cheerful.

"This doesn't look good, Roy." The SP said raising his eyes from the brown case file.

She had been summoned soon after Mrs Bagdi with the help of Constable Chakma had succeeded in booking a room at the Ginger hotel. From the time she walked in, the SP had been assiduously flipping through the pages of the file she had handed over to him.

The inspector stared. She knew he had more to say.

"First, let me start with the basics, here. You want a month old body to be sent for exhumation autopsy. May I know why?" He stared in mock amusement.

"To get any lead that might be of help."

"Do you know that we need to run our appeal through a magistrate to send it for an autopsy? The police don't order or conduct exhumation autopsy."

"Yes, sir. I understand."

"If you don't find anything, we will look like fools." He clicked his tongue.

She remained silent.

"You should just hand over the body to the aunt. You don't need to get all scruffy on your first case--"

"Sir, we suspect foul play." She raised her voice a bit.

"Who are *we*?" He scowled at the woman he had entrusted with an important case. And who in the light of current events was making him second guess his decision.

"SI Das, Constable Chakma and I—"

"You can't rely on the hunch of your deputies, Roy. You must take a call." The SP said sternly.

"I suspect foul play, sir." She said with conviction. "We need to exhume the body to find the cause of death."

"Okay, if you insist. Hope you understand that if nothing comes out of the autopsy, it will make you look ridiculous."

She gazed with unblinking eyes.

Clearing his throat, the SP said in a condescending tone. "Don't forget to seal the site. Once the team of forensic pathologists is formed, they will visit the place and examine the soil in and around the burial site."

She nodded.

"Good. How are things otherwise?" He said in a matter-of-fact tone.

She knew this casual question was anything but casual. "Fine, sir." She said curtly.

He laughed. "Trust doesn't come easily to you, does it, Roy?"

"I don't know what you mean, sir."

"How are things with SI Das?"

"Fine, sir." The inspector answered promptly. She wanted this conversation to end.

"Look, you have just started in the Homicide division. Don't be so harsh on yourself. It's okay to reach out and take advice from your seniors who have been in this game for years." He smiled self-importantly.

"I will remember that, sir." She leapt up from the wooden chair she had been sitting on ramrod straight.

"Wait." He cried. "What does your famous intuition say about this case?"

Inspector Jui Roy was known for her uncanny clairvoyance in the Agartala police circuit. It had helped her in resolving robberies, petty thefts, heists, illegal trafficking and several other crimes. Although she saw it as a combination of observation, intuition and logical deduction, her colleagues viewed it as something akin to ESP or the sixth sense.

"We don't have an autopsy report, yet. No fingerprint report either. The deceased's phone is missing. All we know based on preliminary search and investigation is that the victim was murdered on 21 November. Unless we make a breakthrough and get a few witnesses to testify...a lot is lurking in the dark, still." She sputtered to a halt vexed with herself.

"I know that this case is in capable hands. My only suggestion would be: *go with your hunch.* Override the SI and constable and don't feel bad about it. You *are* their boss." He reassured.

She remained silent. It wrecked her nerves to do so.

"One more thing, Roy. Don't go around scaring school children. They need not bear the brunt of a murder."

Inspector Roy tilted her chin in a rebellious stance. "When a crime is committed, sir, everyone associated with the murdered, directly or indirectly *bears the brunt.* I'll go home and change into something bright and cheerful for Father Joseph and his children." She saluted her amused boss before clomping out.

CHAPTER XVI

Rituparna's Diary

February, 2018

Jha Sir doesn't like me. I can see that. He grunts, snorts or whispers when I am not looking. Grimaces when I smile and answers brusquely when I attempt to make conversation. I've tried to befriend him but whenever we are in the same space, I can feel a bristling animosity pulsating from him. There is no way to undo how he has painted me in his head.

The human mind is a jailhouse, the key to which is hidden in our sweaty fists.

Jha Sir doesn't understand. I had no plans of giving Maths tuitions or competing with him. But, the students insisted. Particularly, Paul. He is a persistent young man. A rebel and a genius. I think he knows it too. That's why he spends most of his time alone. Away from his classmates at his desk, drawing or reading.

He paints well. He showed me a few of his paintings. Most of it was human faces encapsulating in layers of vibrant colours, their joy and sorrow. I think sorrow fascinates him more than joy. The unequal ratio of the joyful versus melancholic faces painted in bright shades of blue, grey and green on his sketchbook tells me so.

He comes home for tuitions along with a batch of nine students on Saturdays and Sundays. There are six boys and four girls in the group. I teach them for two hours in the morning from 9 to 11 a.m. During those hours the house is filled with loud chatter and laughter.

Sometimes I've to ask them to hush their voices lest the neighbours come complaining. Thankfully until now, our next door neighbours have been indifferent to the weekly ruckus.

Even in the group, Paul remains distant. He barely talks. To pull him out of his shell, I keep throwing complex numerical sums at him. When everyone else in the group falls silent over a mathematical sum, his eyes glimmer like a firefly and a flicker of a smile undulates on his otherwise deadpan face.

Eagerly, he pores over his notebook scribbling at a breakneck speed until he can find the solution. Once done, he hands his notebook over to me and starts nibbling on his nails. I keep my gaze down but from the corner of my eyes, I can see him chewing his half-nipped nails with fury. When I beam, "Good job, Paul!" His eyes light up again and for a second that impassive face of his, transforms into the face of an eager young boy keen to impress his guru.

I wonder about his family and the kind of home he hails from. I've not met his parents. They never turn up to pay my monthly tuition fee. Never attend parent-teacher-meetings. The remaining nine in the group come from middle class families. A few richer than the others.

Paul pays me the tuition fee in cash every month on the second without fail. Whenever I ask him about his family, he says they are busy. He does carry a mobile phone like the rest. But, it barely rings.

At times, after his friends have departed, he stays behind and asks me questions about mathematicians and mathematical philosophers. We talk about Euler, Archimedes, Gauss and Conway.

Weeks ago, The Game of Life theory of Conway got him animated and livid. For days we discussed its advantages and loopholes. One day, while we were discussing the Greek mathematicians Archimedes and Aristotle, he remarked,

"*Aristotle was a philosopher.*"

"*And a mathematician,*" *I said.* "*Did you know there was another named Hypatia, a female Greek mathematician?*"

He shook his head negatively. "*She was brilliant. Never married. Dedicated her life to the singular and higher pursuit of science. Do you know what became of her?*"

He stared.

"*She was murdered by religious bigots.*"

His eager face hardened.

"*Women can crunch numbers too you see.*" *I smiled trying to lighten the mood, which had grown sombre due to the mention of murder.*

"*Who said they can't?*" *He held my gaze for a moment.*

When it came to discussing our inner life or family, however, the conversation was lopsided. I found myself talking incessantly and him listening intently. Without contributing much.

One day, while we were discussing life and Maths, he quite abruptly blurted, "*Why are you here?*"

"*To teach,*" *I murmured.*

"*You could have taught in any other place. Why here?*"

I avoided his penetrating gaze. "*You should leave now. I've to prepare for tomorrow's class.*"

"*What are you hiding?*" *He whispered. His eyes still on me.*

"*My private life is not your business. When you open up about yourself let me know.*" *I stood up.*

Picking his black school bag from the floor he walked out, his shoulders stooping. His head bent down. Leaving me to wonder whether I had been too harsh on the introverted teenager. The next day at school, I found him staring fixedly at me. I tried paying no heed to his pregnant stares.

At home, he didn't attempt to solve the sums. I made it a point to ignore him too. After all, he was a smart student

*capable of solving complex problems on his own. The rest --
not-so-bright learners needed my attention. I showered it on
them wholeheartedly without feeling guilty.*

*A week passed. Yesterday, when he came for tuitions, he
kept his gaze averted. For the first time, I didn't task him with
a problem. Instead, I focussed on the others. I could see that
his groupmates were puzzled by this sudden change.*

*They kept stealing glances and exchanging wry smiles.
Once the session came to an end and it was time to leave, like
every other day he stayed behind.*

"Not going home?" I asked.

"I want to tell you something."

I looked at his nervous face.

*"Don't share it with any other teacher or anyone else." He
murmured. His eyes fixed on the white tiled floor.*

"I won't."

"I see colours." His voice was barely a whisper.

*"What?" "I see colours...and forms...in numbers." He raised
his gaze.*

I nodded encouragingly.

"Each number is coloured and...and...in a shape—"

"You mean, textured?"

*"Yes. One is red and pointy. Two is blue and blunt. Three
is yellow and roundish. Four is pink and lean and so on..." He
paused. "I've seen numbers in colours and shapes since I was a
child."*

"You see colours only in numbers?"

"Even people are coloured."

I smiled. "What colour am I?"

"Red. You are always red." He held my gaze.

*"Is that why you don't talk to your classmates? You think
you are different."*

He clenched his jaw.

"You are fine. There is a name for this neurological condition. It's called Synaesthesia."

He scrunched his brows. "Am I a retard?"

"It's not a mental disorder. Only a blending of senses, which creates a heightened sensory experience. When you see something or someone, your brain assigns a colour to it. A shape or form too. What you are experiencing is a form of Synaesthesia—"

"I am a weirdo!" He hissed.

"No. You are a synesthete. That's what people like you are called. And there are many across the world. About 2-4 percent and that's only the official figure." I smiled.

He didn't.

"You are not alone, Paul."

He unclenched his jaw. His face softened. I waited for him to speak up.

"When I learned to count, I saw colours."

"Who taught you to count?"

"No one. I could do it by myself. All I needed were numbers. If I multiplied 65 with 7, then 6 and 5 became two different colourful forms which melded together to become 455 – a vibrant image with its own unique colours and character."

"Who taught you to read?" I asked this time.

"No one—"

"I am guessing you learned to read by yourself."

He nodded.

"Do you see colours in letters too?"

"Yes, but not as bright and well-shaped as in numbers."
He squeezed his lips crossly. Opening up wasn't easy for him. "When I got admitted to the Rainbow School, I was hopeful. I thought maybe now, I'll finally meet those like me."

I knew what was coming but I let him continue.

"*Like a moron, I had asked a boy in class if he saw colours in numbers.*" *He scoffed.* "*He went and told everyone in school that the new boy was a psycho. A psycho!*" *His voice quavered. His palms were clenched into tight fists.*

"*Well, they are wrong. You're not a psycho but a gifted boy.*" *I gently touched his hands. He unclenched his fists. Together we sat in silence until he broke it by saying,* "*Please don't ignore me again.*"

"*I wasn't ignoring—*"

"*You were.*" *Hoisting his bag off the floor he dashed out of the door before I could say more.*

CHAPTER XVII

The Rainbow School

The non-smiling young security guard at the entrance doesn't stop the duo. Father Joseph had ordered him not to. Together they amble in noticing every little thing around them. Dressed in a white sari with golden borders and a bright peacock blue blouse, her hair clipped to the back of her head with a golden hair clip -- something her mother insisted that she don, Inspector Roy looked every inch a young teacher about to take a class.

The SI was dressed in a white shirt and blue jeans. His sartorial staple for occasions like this – when wearing the uniform was not an option. If it were up to him, he would be in uniform three sixty-five days. Often he slept in it too. Particularly on Saturday nights, when he went home late after a night of drinks with his school friends.

A grey cemented pathway winded towards a tall, white fountain at the centre of the ostentatious Christian school which expanded in every direction. A lofty white building with blue-stained windows dazzled under the bright daylight. A loud chatter of school children emanated from inside the building.

"Classes are going on." The SI noted.

The inspector raised her head and noticed the arched golden rainbow atop the school building. "True to its name, it has a bronze rainbow, not a Christian statuette." She murmured.

He followed her gaze. "Rainbows are about hope and optimism. VIBGYOR, the seven colours of the rainbow. We used to learn in school..." His voice trailed off as a group of white and blue-uniformed students ran towards the football field shrieking in excitement.

Tucked away from the bustling centre of the town, the Rainbow School had become popular as one of the best academic institutions in the whole of north-eastern India. The local populace viewed it as a school for the affluent. The yearly fees ran in lakhs, which the school claimed was needed to maintain its auditoriums, football and basketball fields and its academic, administrative and support staff.

Parents whose children secured admission to the upmarket school took pride and boasted about it to their friends and relatives.

"I wish I had studied at a place like this." The SI muttered under his breath as they entered the spacious hallway painted in the hues of the sky – blue and white.

"I loved my school." The inspector said with a tinge of pride in her voice. "Whatever I am today, I am because of my teachers."

"Yes, it all sounds great when you say it like that. But, the truth is I still can't afford many things—"

"Like what?" She snapped.

"Marriage." He blurted.

She stopped in her tracks. "You can't or you won't? There's a difference."

"It's not like that..." His voice trembled. Nervously, turning his gaze, he let it linger on her moon-shaped face. He wanted to say more, much more. To lay bare his heart and confide about every odd thought that had run through his mind for days and nights after their painful separation.

When he tried opening his mouth to form the words, his nerves ran truant. Only a stutter surfaced. "I-I-I never..."

The sudden intensity of his otherwise friendly eyes unnerved her. "I wanted to ride my scooty. You insisted that we travel on your bike. We don't have to make it more difficult for ourselves than it already is." She babbled breaking the moment.

He took a deep breath. "Get your scooty next time then—"

"I will." She said flatly scuttling towards the staffroom and wondering why she had spurted nonsense.

* * *

The staffroom was in a frenzy when the cops walked in. The recess bell had rung only seconds ago. A flurry of scents and loud chatter engulfed Inspector Roy and SI Das. It was lunchtime and everyone was digging into their boxes with gusto.

The inspector cast a sweeping glance at the men and women seated across two long wooden tables in a large rectangular room. There were three mid-sized windows, a metre apart, on one side of the room.

The women were dressed in bright blue saris with emerald green borders and the men sported cobalt blue shirts and black trousers. Father Joseph stood at the centre of the room smiling condescendingly at one and all.

Paying no heed to his presence, the teachers continued to eat and converse like every other day. This was their hour and the principal was in their room.

"Let me make the introductions." He turned to the cops. They nodded. Clearing his throat, he raised his voice. "Teachers. May I've your attention please?"

Some of the teachers looked up at the tall, old man with the long beard and salt and pepper hair reluctantly. The others continued to talk and munch.

"This is Inspector Roy." He tilted his chin towards the inspector. The female teachers tried evaluating the woman.

They noticed her overly straight posture and her calm demeanour. She exuded a kind of morbid sobriety.

"And this is SI Das." He smiled at the man who certainly seemed more amiable. The SI returned his smile.

"You are aware of the unfortunate death of one of our ex-teachers, Rituparna Bagdi. May her soul rest in peace!" The father drew an imaginary cross in the air. "They will be asking you questions about her. As part of her extended family and as responsible citizens, we must do our best to aid the police to catch the culprit." He smiled again at his teachers.

This time none smiled. A gloomy silence had descended over the room. The mention of death at lunchtime! The inspector smiled to herself. The SI cast a furtive glance at his boss. He noticed the sly smile playing on her lips.

She is laughing at her jokes, which no mortal walking on this planet will ever get to hear!

"Inspector, you may begin." The principal ended his short speech and flailed his long arm towards his staff. "Sure, Father. You may leave. I am sure that several things need your attention." She said dismissively.

"Of course." He mumbled perfunctorily unhappy about not being able to have the last word.

"Can we take them to the auditorium for questioning?" The SI asked as the principal turned to leave. "Some of them might not be comfortable talking in here."

"I will get it opened for you. Anything else?"

"That would be all. Thank you, Father." The SI smiled while the inspector's eyes fell on a large-framed woman gawking at her.

Dipti.

"Let's begin with Dipti." She tilted her head towards the woman sitting in the centre of the room surrounded by several colourful boxes of food on her table. "Bring her to the auditorium."

The SI followed the inspector's gaze.

CHAPTER XVIII

Dipti

Dipti Patel sat in the front row of the sprawling auditorium. Her large, kohl-lined eyes were fixed on the enormous wooden stage. Mina di was cleaning the stage slowly with her long blue sweeping stick, making sure not an inch of the surface remained dirty. Her beige sari brightened by a parrot green border added a dash of colour to her otherwise unremarkable drape.

The scrawny old woman had pleated the sari perfectly and appeared at ease in her help-staff uniform. Apparently, it seemed like nothing had changed. Maybe nothing had changed. It was just another day at work.

Dipti sighed. Only months ago, Ritu had been on stage smiling with the kids. Answering their innumerable questions. Instructing the teachers. Managing every little thing deftly. Dipti had never seen her come out of her shell the way she did during the Annual Day celebration.

Inspector Roy considered the voluptuous woman seated before her on a blue plastic chair. Her long hair was neatly tied into a back plait. The long red beaded necklace that decorated her frame heaved as she sighed again.

"Was this a place Rituparna visited frequently?" The inspector asked.

Dipti shook her head. "We were preparing for the Annual Day only months ago."

"When was the Annual Day?" The SI held the voice recorder a little away from Dipti.

"27 October," Dipti answered tartly staring at the recorder.

"Standard procedure. So that we don't miss out on anything important." He explained about the nifty device in his hand, which resembled a dwarfed TV remote control. Dipti shrugged dismissively.

"It was a Saturday. Usually, we celebrate it on a weekend so that the students can rest on Sunday."

"Tell me a bit more about the Annual Day?" The inspector said conversationally.

"You want to know about Rituparna, don't you?" Dipti was in no mood to chat.

Inspector Roy stared. "Sure. But, we do have a system." She said firmly. "Why don't you start with introducing yourself first and then, we will talk about the deceased?"

SI Das snickered. Jui sure knew how to cut someone short.

"I am Dipti Patel and I teach Social Science to classes six to ten."

"Are you from Agartala or did you shift here recently?" The SI asked.

"I am from here. My husband hails from Ahmedabad."

"Interesting. Where did the two of you meet?"

"We met online."

"What does your husband do?"

"How is that relevant to the case?" Dipti cocked her head up.

"Is your husband unemployed?" The inspector paid no attention to her taking umbrage.

"No, he is most certainly not. He runs a business—"

"What kind of business?" The SI snapped.

"He owns a garment shop," Dipti muttered.

"Where?" "City Centre, Melar Math. He owns a shop there."

"Tell us a bit about your family." The inspector softened her tone.

"I live with my husband. My parents live in 79 Tilla and my in-laws live in Ahmedabad. They visit us often."

"Did you study in Tripura?"

"Yes. I studied at the MBB College."

"Where did Rituparna study?"

"Ritu--Rituparna studied at the Presidency University in Kolkata."

"Right." The inspector looked at the time on her phone. It was 2.30 p.m. already. "Father Joseph tells me that she managed an event here--"

"The Annual Day, the one I had mentioned earlier. She did a great job. Everyone was impressed with her. Teachers, parents, students, even the help staff. It was one of the best functions in the history of the Rainbow School."

"Did Paul play a part in the event?"

Dipti's face changed. "Why?" Her voice dropped to a whisper.

"Just curious." The inspector tried sounding casual.

"Paul didn't participate in the main event but he did contribute as a volunteer."

"What did he do as a volunteer?"

"Guided the parents to their seats and helped the teachers and participants."

"Why did he not participate?"

"He never does. He is an introvert. Stays away from attention. Doesn't like being on stage." "Stage fright?" The SI suggested.

"No. He doesn't like to work in a team. He shines when he is left alone to his devices." Dipti explained.

"Why are we discussing him? I thought you wanted to know about Ritu?"

"We do. Tell us more about her." The inspector half-smiled. Dipti reflected her smile. "Ritu and I were friends. Although I did most of the talking, she wasn't exactly the silent kind. She spoke when it mattered, and she always knew when to speak up."

"She was an English teacher, wasn't she?"

"Yes."

"Then why did she teach Maths?"

"The students insisted. They loved her in class. She had a brilliant mind that did not like whiling away time in idle gossip. When she was free, she would rush to the library and read there for hours. Often forgetting about her classes."

"She wasn't exactly teaching Maths in school, she was giving private tuitions after school." The SI scoffed.

"What's wrong with that? We all do. If we don't, the parents insist—"

"It's a good way to earn an extra income." He smirked.

"Even the traffic police harass people to earn an extra income." Dipti countered.

"Not all policemen are corrupt." The SI narrowed his eyes.

"Not all teachers are tuition mongers either."

"Do you know that Indian families spend Rs 25,000 crore on tuition per year? And in Tripura 87 % students take tuitions, second only to West Bengal." The SI's agitated voice whipped. "It's a well-oiled business." He added suggestively.

Dipti threw an insolent look at the cop. "I wish I had some figures too on the Indian police. All I can say is that Rituparna didn't provide tuitions for money. She only wanted to help."

A pregnant silence followed.

Eventually, Inspector Roy cleared her throat. "How was she with the other teachers? Was there anyone in particular who didn't like Ritu?"

Dipti shifted her seething gaze from the SI to his boss, tempering a little. "No one liked her. They were all jealous of her. The day they heard of her resignation, they said she must have run away with a man—"

"Why? Was there any particular reason to think that way?"

"Of course, not." Dipti cried. "Why would you say that?"

"Not being judgemental. We are just trying to explore every possibility."

Dipti considered the inspector. There was something different about the woman that she couldn't really fathom. An unusual calm and an unforthcoming demeanour. Oddly, she reminded her of...Ritu.

"She was a divorcee," Dipti shrugged. "Why do we always presume that unattached women are promiscuous?"

The inspector smiled wryly. "I am a divorcee."

"Oh. Then you must know..."

SI Das cast a furtive glance at his boss. He didn't know where this was going or if he should just turn the recorder off and leave the auditorium. Perplexed, he stood rooted to the ground. "Dipti, take your time and think." The inspector leaned closer. "Did you notice something that struck you as odd or did Ritu confide in you about anything confidential that might help us with finding her killer?"

The SI smiled to himself. The interrogation was back on track.

"I think Ritu had a strange relationship with her ex-husband." Dipti said after a pause. "Mrinal Chatterjee, you mean?"

"Right. He called her often. Came down to meet her. He was always trying to...you know...get closer."

"It seems to me that he was in love with her." The SI supplied.

"Maybe—" "What about Rituparna?" The inspector interjected.

"At times it felt like she loved him too. But, sometimes it felt like she detested him."

"Why did they get divorced?" He cut in.

"I had asked her about it. A long, painful story better left alone. She had said brushing it off with a smile."

The inspector thought about it for a moment. "Do you have pictures of the Annual Day event on your phone?"

Dipti shook her head enthusiastically. "I do. I've many other pictures. I wanted to delete them. When you lose someone dear, their pictures only cause pain." She said searching through her phone, which she had been clutching all along.

For the next several minutes' Inspector Roy and SI Das browsed through countless pictures trying to find a clue, a hint to arrange the pieces of the mystery in a logical pattern.

"You know the day after the event, I wanted to gift her something instead of simply congratulating her. She had done such a fabulous job. Frantically, I searched online and then decided on gifting her a book. The Man Who Knew Infinity by Kanigel. I wrapped it in a special red and white paper." Dipti smiled fondly.

"She never told me, but later I came to realise that she had already read the book. Ritu was an avid reader."

When Dipti stood up to leave, the inspector asked, "How was her relationship with Virendra Jha?"

"Sour."

"What do you mean?"
"He detested her."
"And she?"
"She wanted to build a bridge."
"Did she succeed?"
Dipti flipped her long plait jiggling out.

CHAPTER XIX

Virendra Jha

A stout and short man with glasses placed firmly on his bulbous nose sat staring at the duo. His pate half-filled with hair was parted meticulously at the centre. A sigh escaped now and then from his puckered lips. His wispy moustache undulated as he exhaled and inhaled air noisily.

The cobalt blue shirt that he was wearing like all the other male teachers in the school was covered with chalk powder in parts. SI Das disliked the man instantly. There was something vile and repulsive about his smug face. If he were not a teacher he may as well be a petty criminal. A bootlegger perhaps.

"I've got a class at 3.15. My last class. We will need to hurry up." He said ceremoniously.

"The deceased mentioned you in her diary. She said that you had misbehaved with her. I hope you understand that this is no ordinary interrogation and you are not in a job interview." Inspector Roy said in an imperious tone.

Jha's face altered suddenly. "I've caused her no harm. I was on good terms with Rituparna."

"Cut the crap, Jha." SI Das barked. "Tell us the truth. From the beginning."

The SI's words rattled him. He squirmed in his chair. Collecting his thoughts, he began shakily, "My name is Virendra Jha and I teach Mathematics to all classes -- six to twelve. I have been working in this school since 2008. I was working in the Hindi School earlier. But, Father Joseph offered a good hike." Jha rambled nervously in Hindi-laced English.

"You are not from here, are you?" The SI shifted the voice recorder from one hand to the other.

"I am from Jamshedpur. My family lives there."

"Your family?"

"My wife and two sons. They didn't want to come here."

"Where do you live?"

"I live inside the campus next to the boy's hostel."

"There is a hostel here?" The inspector scrunched her eyes.

"Yes, for the resident students."

"You live in the teacher's quarters?"

"There is a room next to the boy's hostel with a toilet and a small kitchen. I live there and look after them."

"You are the hostel in charge?" She drawled.

He nodded. "That way I don't have to pay rent."

"Don't you give tuitions?"

"I have to make money somehow. My elder son is in class ten. He goes for IIT coaching and it's expensive."

He looked at the inspector and then at the SI expecting a kind word or a sympathetic nod – none came. Frowning he continued, "I don't like living here. I want to go home. Back to my family—"

"Yet, you can't because you earn a lot more here. In Jamshedpur, there are many Math teachers like you." The inspector cut in.

Jha glared. He didn't like the woman at all.

"Rituparna Bagdi was giving tuitions too. Before her death of course." The SI chimed in.

"She wasn't a good teacher. She thought she was but she wasn't."

"Interesting." The inspector retorted. "Why do you think so?"

"She skipped chapters without any reason. Jumped from the first to the very last. There was no pattern in the way she taught. No method. Also, she never made them solve IIT practice papers unless the students asked for it."

"Is that so?" The SI suppressed a laugh.

Jha composed himself. "Mathematics is not madness. We must approach it methodically. Not all students are like Paul."

The inspector chuckled. "Exactly. Not everyone is a prodigy."

It took Virendra Jha a while to grasp the import of her words and the accompanying sarcasm.

"Tell us about Paul. You have been teaching him for ten years, I assume?"

"No, no." Jha paused. "I mean...he came to the Rainbow School only two years ago."

"Go on." The SI prodded.

"Paul, as you put it, is a prodigy. He knows it too. He won't say it but we all know that he is quite proud of it. He thinks he is better than the rest. I have seen him staring at the others in the class with an air of superiority. When I ask him a question, he takes his time to respond. At times, he pretends like he hasn't heard." The Maths teacher explained. His eyes were somewhere distant.

"Is he disrespectful?" The inspector offered.

"Highly. No one likes him. Neither his peers nor his teachers. Although his peers seek his approval for everything."

"In what way?" SI Das pulled a plastic chair out and sat next to the teacher with his recorder in hand.

"Once, the twelfth standard wanted a free class to study for their Chemistry practical, which was supposed to happen in the next class. Whereas I needed to finish the chapter on Statistics so I asked them not to. They insisted. I didn't know what to do. Suddenly, Paul stood up explaining how Statistics was much more important than a Chem practical. Everyone magically agreed." His lips curved into a disdainful smile.

The inspector reflected on that for a moment before saying, "Did he prefer Rituparna's teaching over yours?"

"Rituparna Bagdi had no experience in teaching Maths. She was a fluke." He ran his fingers over his moustache. "And flukes don't last." He hissed spitefully.

"Where were you on 21 November?" The SI cut to the chase.

"That was a month ago."

"Think hard because that was the day Rituparna was killed and buried in her backyard."

Jha looked at the cops in bewilderment. His eyes darting from one to the other. "I didn't kill her. Why would I kill her?" He yelped.

"She was eating a large chunk of your tuitions." The SI levelled.

"They have all returned to me. It wasn't their fault. They were misguided by Paul."

"Can you give us the names of those students who took tuitions from Rituparna Bagdi?"

"Of course." Jha beamed for the first time. Promptly, he dictated the names of the nine students. SI Das wrote it down on a sheet of paper.

When Jha was done, the inspector threw a bait. "Paul thought Rituparna was a better teacher—"

"That boy was smitten by her." He scoffed.

"What do you mean?"

"Here." Jha took his phone out. Browsing through the picture gallery, he pulled out an image. Thrusting the scuffed smartphone at the SI, he whispered, "Look."

In the picture, Rituparna was seen talking to a lanky tribal boy.

"Look, at this one."

In the next picture, the boy was seen holding her hand. They looked like they were having an argument.

"I took this picture on Annual Day. They were having an affair, ma'am." He snorted.

"Send these pictures to SI Das." She commanded. "Why were you spying on them?"

"I was going to the toilet. I saw them standing at the corner, near the green room."

The inspector arched an eyebrow in disapproval. "This doesn't prove your innocence."

"I did not kill her. I've got a family to look after. What would happen to them if I land up in jail?" He reasoned. The cops stared at him calmly. "Also, I was in my room on 21 November. You can ask the students or check the CCTV footage."

"We will go through the footage for sure." The SI warned.

"Sir, I hated that woman but I didn't kill her. I didn't. You have to believe me." Jha swayed his stodgy arms in the air exasperatedly.

CHAPTER XX

Rituparna's Diary

March, 2018

I've finally started to smile again. Often, I catch myself gurgling happily in class. My students compliment me by saying, "Ma'am you look so pretty today. You should wear yellow more often."

I know it has nothing to do with the colour of my fabric or my facial features. Rather it's about finding happiness in the little somethings. The joy of discovering life in the tiny and the trivial. I've never been this cheerful in years.

I don't know if it's Agartala or the fact that I've summoned enough courage to snap a tie, which had pushed me into seeking asylum in an unknown town in the first place.

With Mrinal, life was intense and difficult. His temper altered between hot and sizzling. He was always looking for a spark in relationships, conversations, people and life. What he didn't make room for was the uncharismatic and the mundane.

It's strange how we all change. How the prism through which we view people adjusts itself with time.

Now, when I am no longer with him – he seems tolerable. Even appealing. Not that he wasn't captivating earlier. He was always a hit with women. His sulky demeanour, tall frame, the mysterious timbre of his resonating voice and his seething brown eyes, which turned slightly green in the light made my heart flutter too.

We met at Nandan during an International film festival. I was standing in the queue waiting to watch a Japanese film

84

named Confessions – a story of a teacher who goes about taking revenge on her students for killing her little daughter.

We were both unaccompanied and sat next to each other watching the film together. Must have been providence. Why else would a student pursuing a Master's in Mathematics land up next to an aspiring actor?

When the film ended, he turned toward me and said, "Brilliant."

"I guess," I murmured.

"You didn't like it?"

"I did. It was a good break."

"You liked the film, but you didn't love it. Why?" He turned that burning gaze on me. The theatre was half empty. Most people had left.

"I was in awe of Kanae Minato's book. And..." I averted my gaze.

His eyes were on fire.

"I was supposed to watch the film with a friend. She didn't turn up. It was her idea." I picked my bag up from the empty seat on which Meena was supposed to sit – if her doctor boyfriend hadn't shown up and insisted that she spent the evening with him.

"You've read the book?" He was in no mood to end the conversation.

"Why is that surprising?" I stood up stepping towards the aisle.

"Not many have."

"How can I be blamed for that?" I smiled.

"Since this movie failed to impress, we must watch another... film." He followed.

"Why?" I turned around.

His thick black unkempt hair that touched the nape of his neck and his lazy, smoky gaze made my heart race.

"*I want to try and change your opinion.*"

"*Why does it matter?*"

"*What?*" *He leaned lessening the distance between us.*

"*My opinion. Why would that matter to you?*" *I whispered.*

"*I don't know.*" *He ran his long fingers through his hair and chuckled -- exposing his dimples.*

After that day we met often to watch films. Sometimes, we met along with his friends. He had innumerable male and female friends although he barely spoke. Mostly he grunted and gave his opinion only when asked to.

Despite being appreciated and included, I found him staring at me wistfully from across the room at parties and gatherings. At times, he simply abandoned his friends in the middle of a conversation snuggling closer to me.

"*Are you drunk?*" *I would whisper.*

"*How does it matter?*" *He would drawl in a low voice.*

"*It matters to me. Drunk men can't be trusted.*"

"*Then I am not drunk.*" *He would lace his fingers with mine and close his eyes. Breathing deeply.*

He came from money and wasted a lot of it on his friends. Many borrowed from him never bothering to return. When I pointed that out to him, one starlit evening, he pulled me close and whispered into my years, "*Marry me then.*"

"*What do you mean?*"

"*Marry me and save me from them.*"

"*Mrinal!*"

"*Rituparna! I am serious.*"

"*I've to ask my aunt.*"

"*I've to ask my parents, but if you say yes — nothing or no one can come in between.*"

"*I've to complete my Master's.*" *I was still in shock.*

"*Then do. Who's stopping you?*"

"*I want to do another Masters.*" *My voice trembled. My head spun.*

"*Do as many as you want. Just marry me.*"

My aunt hated him the moment she set his eyes on him. His parents accepted me reluctantly. I may have been an extraordinary student but, I was still from the lowest caste. And my fledgling actor-husband was a Brahmin boy.

"*They will come around.*" *He shrugged.*

"*I don't think so.*" *I sighed.*

After marriage, I moved into his large parental home at Shoba Bazaar. It had been decked with lights, the day we moved in. Garlands made of red roses and white, fragrant tuberoses hung from the terrace. After all, the only son of a Zamindari family doesn't get married every day.

My aunt gave me a bunch of jewellery in gold and silver. She didn't have much. But that didn't stop her from spending her last saved rupee on a niece who had done nothing for her in return.

Living in the Chatterjee household was daunting. My short but fine-looking mother-in-law was either silent or scornful. Her jibes were mostly directed at the mediocrity of my features and my incredible luck at having bagged a handsome, rich and high-caste boy from a respectable family. Although her snide remarks did offend me in the beginning, with time I came to ignore her vileness and focused on academics instead. To my credit, I post graduated with a top score in Mathematics and took admission to pursue a Masters in English.

My father-in-law was a quiet man who kept to himself. He spent half of his waking hours in his room trading in stocks through a desktop. In the remaining hours, he read about stock trading and finance. He had acquired a large inheritance from his ancestors and by trading regularly, he had increased his wealth by leaps and bounds.

Convinced that this was the best way to augment his capital, he sat on a wooden armchair glued to his computer clicking on his mouse all day. Despite his peculiar ways, which he never cared to explain, my father-in-law paid my college fees. His son never did.

Mrinal and I spent two tumultuous years around them, under the same roof. Heated arguments, cold distances and passionate nights kept us together. His mercurial mood and drunken bouts were amplified by his failure at garnering auditions and roles.

Despite his attempts to enter the film circuit, he didn't shine. He got bit roles but was never noticed or appreciated. I saw him hiding away at home for days in his room. His mother crying helplessly and his tall, thin father stooped outside his room, staring blankly. Unsure of everything.

Mrinal opened the door for no one, except me. I walked in carrying a glass of cold lemonade, a truce drink, while he stood next to the door, ready to bang it shut over his frazzled parents. He was like an ailing child who refused to come to terms with the reality of his situation.

One afternoon, he got a call for an audition. I had just returned from the university after a day of back-to-back classes. He pulled me close as soon as I walked through the coffee brown creaky wooden gate of his home. "What do you think?" He was wearing a new sky blue shirt and a pair of black jeans.

"You are shining. Where are you off to?"

"I will be back in a few hours."

"All the best," I said.

"How did you know?"

I kissed his forehead. "Give your best."

Later that night, when he staggered into the room, I could smell liquor all over him. I said nothing. I knew he didn't get the part but I didn't want to prick a wound. Sitting up on the bed, I waited for him to speak. He avoided my gaze.

"Are you hungry?" I said after a while.

Flinging his shoes away, he tottered towards me. His eyes had turned icy. When he plonked on the bed next to me, my heart thumped wildly.

"Do you want something to eat?" I heard myself whisper. He didn't answer. Instead, he grabbed my arms pinning them on the bed.

"I don't want to," I whispered.

"Mrinal, look at me." He met my eyes.

"It's not the end of the world."

"It is." He pressed his lips over mine. His breath stank of liquor. His eyes were not of the man I had loved. Dearly. I tried pulling away.

Reasoned. Pleaded. Mollified. He refused to budge. Tasting and tearing me with fury and vehemence, I had never encountered or expected, he continued to storm his way into me. I quivered beneath him in fear and disgust. Every inch of my body riled up in protest. When he was done, he flipped over, turning the lights off.

In the darkness of the room paying no heed to the numbness of my limbs and flesh, I discarded my clothes and grabbed a bag. Dazedly, in the middle of the night, dressing up in god-knows-what and with a hundred rupee note in my purse, I walked out.

Promising to my bruised and broken self that I would never turn back.

CHAPTER XXI

Paul

Inspector Roy took a good look at the boy. Tall, lithe, tea coloured with short cropped hair, he appeared every inch a schoolboy. Only his mono-lidded eyes, which scanned its surroundings like a prowling cheetah gave a glimpse of a razor sharp mind that Rituparna had mentioned in her diary.

From the time he had walked in and sat on the chair cross-armed, he hadn't spoken.

The inspector tried again. "Your name please?"

"Paul." He replied wearily this time.

"Full name?"

"Paul Jamatia."

"How old are you?"

"Eighteen."

"Where do you live?"

"Near Kali Mandir."

"What about your family?"

"I live with my younger sister."

"Where does she study?"

"She doesn't go to school."

"Why not?"

"She is ill."

"Ill with what?"

"ASD. Autism Spectrum Disorder--"

"I know that." She cut him off. "How old is your sister?"

"Ten years old."

"Who takes care of her in your absence?"

"Neighbours."

"What about your parents?"

He paused. His face impassive. "They died."

"How?"

"In an accident."

"When?"

"When I was six."

"Who pays your school fees?"

"Father Joseph."

"What do you mean?"

"I am a charity case. He has waived my fees."

The inspector tried collecting her thoughts. The principal hadn't mentioned it. "Why did he do that?"

His lips twitched, "He found me promising and wanted to give me a chance."

"Where were you studying before you came to the Rainbow School?"

"I wasn't studying. I was working."

"Where?"

"Dharmanagar."

"What kind of work were you doing?"

"I was working in a tea shop."

"How did you educate yourself then?"

"I studied on my own. My friends helped me from time to time with books."

"Are you still in touch with your friends?"

"No."

"Why not?"

"I've moved on." He said boldly looking straight into her eyes. Inspector Roy shifted in her chair. Wincing under his penetrating gaze.

"What do you think happened to Rituparna Bagdi?" The SI watched the boy closely.

Calmly looking straight into his eyes Paul said, "She was murdered."

"Do you have any idea who might have killed her?"

"Isn't that your job?" He sneered. SI Das clenched his jaw.

Paul's scornful words sliced through her too, but she didn't let it show. "Where were you on 21 November?"

"I was at home with my sister. You can ask my neighbours."

"You think your neighbours will remember where you were a month ago?" The SI snapped.

"Why don't you find out?" He shrugged.

"We will and once we find out – you will have to come up with a solid excuse to expunge yourself." The SI warned.

Paul scrunched his eyes and then broke into a constricted, mock laughter. "You guys are funny, you know that?"

CHAPTER XXII

Rituparna's Diary

April, 2018

After that night, I filed for a divorce. Mrinal called and called. When I paid no heed to his ceaseless calls, he stood knocking on my door for days on end. For weeks, I didn't step out of my home.

Each time he came knocking, my aunt, told him clearly that I didn't want to meet or talk to him. Weeks turned to months. Tired of being locked inside, I finally stepped out to go to college and bumped into him outside my college gate.

"I was drunk." He rasped blocking my way. His eyes burned into mine.

"You are always drunk." I removed my arm from his tight grip walking away. He kept sending texts -- apologizing and explaining, but my heart had frozen that night. I just couldn't open it up to him again.

A few months later, he stopped. Calling. Texting. Apologizing. He even agreed to sign the divorce papers. Maybe he had grown tired of it all. We had an amicable, out-of-court settlement citing incompatibility – a heavy, serious-sounding, inadequate word.

I thought we were free now. Free from the vice-like grip of the past.

When I came here months ago, I was bent on turning a new leaf and making a fresh start. And I had. Although his face, words and his touch continued to haunt me. At times, I longed for his touch. Then like a haunting nightmare, the memory of that night flashed leaving me feeling defiled and dirty.

Oscillating between love, hatred and the infinite emotions in between, my days dimmed into nights. Slowly as the days progressed, the innocuous banter at school and the ready smiles of my students pulled me away from the prickling memories -- making room for sunshine.

One Sunday evening, when the setting sun shot its colours through the endless white sky, an uninvited visitor came knocking on my door.

"May I come in? Please." He begged. His eyes had gone back to being what they were -- soft and melting. I stood holding the door. Half in shock, half in fear.

He whispered. "Please, open the door, Ritu."

"Why?"

"To talk like we used to." Eventually, after minutes of fighting an internal battle, I opened the door.

"You look settled." He said running his gaze all over my room.

"How did you find me?"

"Meena." He smiled feebly plonking on the chair. I stood watching him.

"Why are you here?"

"Make me some lemonade. I missed it." He held my gaze.

"I can't make lemonade for you," I said bluntly.

"Then, let me make some." He lurched up.

"Where are the lemons?"

"Are you here to make lemonade?"

"Not if you don't want me to."

"Mrinal." I stood facing him. My heart thudding in alarm. "What are you doing here?"

"I've got a part in an independent film." He said sheepishly.

"Here? In Agartala?"

He nodded.

"*Is it a paid gig?*" *I blurted out of habit. This is what I used to ask when we were married and he auditioned for roles every other day.*

"*It is.*"

"*Congratulations!*" *A rush of happiness made me smile.*

"*It barely covers the cost of the plane tickets. Must start somewhere.*" *He shrugged dismissively.*

Although I had a niggling suspicion that he was in Agartala to make his way back into my life, I let myself believe that he was indeed turning a new leaf.

"*Put your best foot forward,*" *I said.* "*But, you can't keep dropping here.*"

He laughed, a mirthless, hollow laugh. "*Can we forget the past?*"

"*No,*" *I said listlessly opening the refrigerator and taking some lemons out.*

"*For an hour at least...this evening?*" *He implored.*

I fetched a glass jug and took out the lemon squeezer from the cupboard. "*I thought you were making lemonade.*"

His face broke into a wobbly smile. For the next few hours, we stood next to each other mixing sugar and lime in water and discussing the trivial and pointless. Later that evening, when I said goodbye to him, I also bade farewell to the anguish and fury that I had nursed for long in the darkest corners of my soul.

I chose to forgive him. It was easier to forgive than forget.

CHAPTER XXIII

The Remaining Nine

Father Joseph stood facing the duo. His hands were firmly planted on his bony waist. "I can't send nine students for an interview."

"It's an interrogation, not an interview." The SI said brusquely. He swivelled around in his chair and took a good look at the roman wall clock hanging above his head.

"It's 3 already. The buses leave at 3.30."

"Then we will interview a few today and the rest tomorrow—"

"Again, tomorrow?" He shuddered.

"This is important, Father. Please allow us to do our job." The inspector said mildly.

"This is ludicrous! Why do you need to go around interrogating such a large group? Wasn't talking to Paul enough?"

"All these students knew Rituparna. They may have something crucial to add. Plus, we can't build our report on Paul's testimony."

"Why not?"

"He told us many new things that we weren't informed of earlier."

"Like what?"

"We didn't know that he is a charity case or that his fees have been waived." The inspector said pointedly. Father Joseph swallowed. He knew exactly what the inspector was implying. She was accusing him of hiding information.

"Okay. But, you will need to wind up before 3.30 p.m. The buses won't be held back for this. We don't want parents complaining—"

"Just send these students in." SI Das handed over the sheet with the names to the principal.

The cornered man groaned in frustration – his poise gone. Clutching the sheet of paper, he turned around to make a grand exit.

"One more thing, Father. We will need the CCTV footage of the camera placed above the door to your room." The inspector said pithily.

The principal stopped in his tracks. "Is it necessary? We do have another CCTV camera at the entry and exit gates. Won't that suffice—"

"I am afraid, no." She cut in.

"Focus on his room's CCTV footage, Das." Inspector Roy said when the principal was out of hearing distance.

Student no 1.
Madhu Deb

"Ritu Ma'am was good only. I don't remember her much. We went for tuition at her place for a few months. There were others too, ask them na... We went for two days a week. In the mornings. She made us do sums. Tough sums most of the time. That show-off Paul was always the one to solve them rightly. I could too. Just never tried. I am not interested in Maths na. My mother wanted me to take up Science. I had scored ninety percent in my tenth and yet, I wanted to take up Political Science. I love politicians and politics so much--"

"Who is the governor of Tripura?" The SI asked after listening for ten minutes.

"I don't know. I told you I wanted to take up Pol Science. Now, I am a Science student--"

"It's Ramesh Bais." He said acerbically.

"What did you think of Ritu Ma'am?" Inspector Roy asked in a mollifying tone.

The girl rolled her eyes. "She was weird. Always talked about mathematicians and numbers. Variables and formulae. She never took a break when she taught us. If we asked for a break, she played Math pop quiz!"

"You didn't like her?"

"I never said that. She wasn't like the rest."

"What do you mean?"

"She wasn't like the rest of the teachers."

Student no 2.
Shahid Amin

"She was brilliant. Hands down our best Maths teacher. I was shocked to hear about, you know... We were all shocked. Paul didn't come to school after, you know... He was her favourite student. Although she was never partial to him. She gave us all a chance. At times, when I was able to solve the sums, she congratulated me."

"Did you notice anything unusual at her place? Anything that you may remember?" Inspector Roy asked.

"A few days before we saw Ma'am for the last time, Paul received a weird call. He argued with the caller. I had gone out for a smoke—I mean, I-I...don't smoke." After a hesitant pause, "Please don't tell my parents."

"We have no interest in talking to your parents." The SI assured. "What did Paul say on the call?"

"He said something like, *get someone else to do it. I can't.*"

"Anything else?"

"Nope, just that. When he hung up, he was upset and cursed for a while."

Student no. 3
Mili Majumdar

"Why are you asking about Ritu Ma'am? I wasn't close to her. I didn't even like her. She had a superiority complex. If she was that good what was she doing here in Agartala? She should have gone abroad and done research or something. Or better still -- got into IT. Only losers become teachers these days."

The SI glared. Inspector Roy shook her head resignedly.

"I don't want to waste my time thinking about a dead person. May I leave?"

"What about Paul?" The SI snapped.

"He is an asshole. Thinks too highly of himself too. Her blue-eyed boy."

"Does Paul have a girlfriend?" The inspector said in a casual tone.

"Paul loves himself way too much."

"What makes you say that?"

"Sixth sense."

"Why did you go for tuitions if you didn't like Rituparna Bagdi?" The SI said pointedly.

"My BFFs asked me to. Can I go now?"

Student no. 4
Akash Chakma

"I don't get Maths. Ritu Ma'am made it sound simple. When I took tuitions, I thought I will pass. Now, I don't think I will. Jha Sir, sucks. Don't tell him that, please. He will fail me."

"Why would he do that?" The SI held the recorder in his left hand and rubbed his temple with his right. These teenagers were giving him a headache.

The boy stared at the SI and then looked at the inspector in confusion. She nodded signalling him to continue.

"He is vindictive. If he hears someone saying something bad about him, he takes it out on them."

"How?" She asked gently.

"Gives a tough sum and makes them do it in class. He did that once to Paul. But, Paul whacked his ass. He solved it in no time." A smirk zigzagged across his small face.

"Do they dislike each other?"

"They can't stand each other. But..." The cops waited. "After Ma'am's death, they seem to have thawed."

Next Day Morning

Student no. 5

Deep Debnath

"I don't remember her much. I don't want to miss my Chem class--"

"Didn't you go for tuitions to her home?" The SI interrupted.

"I did but I don't remember her. It was months ago. Also, I missed the last week of tuitions." "Why?"

"Viral fever."

"What did you think of her as a teacher?"

"Nothing. I don't think of teachers. Only Paul does."

"What do you mean?" "He liked her. Even Jha Sir liked her. That's why they hated each other."

"Interesting." The inspector murmured.

"Very. Everyone used to joke about them on WhatsApp."

"You have groups on WhatsApp?"

"Of course! How else will we keep in touch? We've one for each subject. I mean the subjects for which we take tuition."

Student no. 6

Jahnvi Singh

"I joined this school only in class eleventh. I was studying in KV, Kunjaban earlier. My father's in the army. We army kids are different."

"How so?" Inspector Roy was amused.

"We are tough and disciplined. Anyway...I don't like this school much. I miss my friends at KV."

"What don't you like?"

"I don't like my classmates. They are you know... jealous and closed. They have their groups and they won't let me in. I am good at Physics and Math so the girls are jealous of me. The boys are better. They are okay – friendly."

"Do you remember Rituparna Bagdi?"

"Yes, she was sweet to me. I was always the first one to reach her home for tuition. Sometimes, I used to go early to just chat with Ma'am."

"What did you talk about?"

"Basic stuff. School, boys."

"What did she talk about?"

"Mmm...She didn't talk much. She listened. I think once, she mentioned something about her husband."

"What did she say?"

"Men are as complex as women. Don't let them fool you into thinking otherwise. She had said something like that."

"Rituparna was a divorcee."

"I know. I found it odd too."

"Why?"

"It felt like...she was still married."

Student no. 7
Shayanto Bhowmik

"She was a savage. She knew how to cut people off. The students liked her more because of that. She won all arguments. She taught English and she taught Maths. Why would anyone do that unless they want to prove a point?"

"What point?" Inspector Roy squirmed in her chair. Her legs had turned heavy and numb. She wanted to stand up and take a walk around the auditorium. But, doing that would distract the kid. So she stay put.

Her SI was drooping on his chair, his right hand clasped around the recorder.

"Anyone can learn anything. There are no barriers really. No segregation between the so-called Arts and the Sciences." The boy explained excitedly.

"Are you a good student?" She gazed at the bespectacled face who appeared wiser beyond his years.

"You could say. I've been standing first in class since the fifth grade."

"Not Paul?"

"He is only good at Maths and above average in English."

"I see."

"No one gets him. Most avoid him like the flu. I think that's why he bonded with Ritu Ma'am. She understood him."

Student no. 8
Kriti Das

"I was so shaken when I heard about Ma'am. Who would do such a thing and why? She was a nice person. She never scolded us. Even when she raised her voice, which was rarely, she did it for a reason. Only an evil person can kill someone like her. I wish I knew who it was. I did think about it, but I couldn't come up with a name."

"What about Jha Sir?"

"Jha Sir can't kill anyone." The lanky girl with braces giggled. "Why, he is even afraid of a Pomeranian dog!"

Student no. 9
Anil Ganguly

"I think she committed suicide. She was depressed anyway."

The inspector stretched her legs finally standing up.

"Why do you say that?"

"I saw her crying once at school. She had just stepped out of the toilet and I had bumped into her. Her eyes were red and swollen. She was clutching her phone."

"That was once." The SI mumbled straightening up.

"I saw her crying on the Annual Day too. She was on stage and we had just finished our play. She was wiping her eyes."

"Maybe she was touched by your performances—"

"No! We sucked on stage. Some of us forgot our lines. Two dancers collided and fell on stage. The singing was off-tune. Thankfully, our parents cheered and clapped. And everyone thought the Annual Day was a grand success. It wasn't. It never is." The boy smiled with an air of someone who knows what he is talking about.

CHAPTER XXIV

The Puzzle Pieces

"I will see you in an hour." Inspector Roy remarked disembarking from the SI's bike in front of her home. Curtains rustled and stilled in a matter of seconds.

The SI chuckled. "Your mother still spies on the men you date?"

"We are not dating." She said inducing a sudden sternness in her voice.

SI Das stopped smiling. He didn't know why even now, her words slammed his insides. "I've a girlfriend." He muttered looking away.

"The one who keeps stalking you."

"She doesn't stalk me. She loves me." He bristled in defence.

"When are you getting married?" Her riposte riled him but he let it slide.

"Let's talk about the case."

"Sure. We did get a few leads. Although we must proceed with caution." She said in a business-like fashion.

"Leads?" He felt relieved to be talking about the case.

"For one, we know that Jha wasn't her friend. He did hate her. Two, Paul is an enigma. A self-taught prodigy with a past. Three, Paul is a charity case – a fact hidden by the principal. We will have to keep a close eye on Jha and Paul. Also, we will need to dig into Paul's past life."

"Plus, we need to find out why Paul was angered by a call? Who was the caller?"

"Good point, Pritam." She beamed. He returned her smile reluctantly.

"I had almost forgotten. There was an old axe on Sunil Lahiri's property. We didn't find it in our preliminary search. You must ask Lahiri to hand it over to us for fingerprint analysis."

"I didn't know that."

"Rituparna mentions it in her diary." She clarified.

The curtains rustled again. This time a face emerged -- that of an old woman with tired eyes. The SI locked gaze with the woman at the window. None turned their face away. The inspector perceiving the cold vibe intervened, "Okay, will catch you later--"

"Was Rituparna depressed? Why did she cry often in school?" He uttered slowly shifting his gaze towards the woman standing next to him.

"Even if she were, she wouldn't under any circumstance bury herself in her backyard. There are other ways to die. Relatively painless ones." She turned away disappearing into her home.

CHAPTER XXV

Rituparna's Diary

May 2018

Summer vacations must be a welcome relief for the students but for me – it's a drag. I get up early in the morning thinking -- another workday. Within a few seconds, it dawns upon my dazed senses that it's just another day at home.

I had spoken to my aunt a week ago. She had extended what seemed like an invitation to spend the summer months in Kolkata with her. I skirted around the invite. I didn't want to tell her that being there in my hometown would give everyone the licence to remind me of my broken marriage.

To hide from the world and the man who betrayed my trust, I didn't go to Kolkata. Instead, that very man landed on my doorstep. For the past month, he has become a regular visitor and for the life in me, I don't know what to make of it. I've forgiven him, yes, but returning to him is out of the question. I've told him as much as I've no intention of leading him on.

"You don't have to. I won't exert force on you – ever again." *He had assured me.*

To get away from his thoughts, I've started reading more. Books have been keeping me company along with the group of ten students who drop in on the weekends.

They chatter, smile and argue among themselves a lot. Paul is his usual self always. Tight-lipped and inert. A silent virtuoso. He continues to stay behind talking about complex formulae and solutions and solving as many problems as possible.

Last balmy Sunday, sometime after eleven, Mrinal dropped by. All the students had left by then. Only Paul was crouched over my college texts books, leafing through the pages, scribbling and solving in his thick notebook.

I was in the kitchen making pasta for lunch. Paul answered the door letting Mrinal in. They stood staring at each other until I made the introductions.

A spiky silence followed.

"Don't mind me," Mrinal said forcing a smile on his face.

Paul's only response was an icy glare. Later, when he trundled out after an hour, Mrinal looked at me thoughtfully, "You should not let him stay, Ritu."

I was surprised. "Why do you say so?"

"He is into you."

I suppressed a laugh. "Come on. He is a sucker for numbers. Just like me."

"It's more than that. Much more."

"Are you envious of a teenager stealing your thunder?" He smiled awkwardly at my warm tone.

"Listen, Ritu. You don't have anyone here. I will be leaving soon. Maybe a week or more. Be careful. That's all I am saying."

"Do you know why I took a job here in Agartala?"

He looked at me uneasily. "To get away from you. So stop being worried on my behalf. It defies logic."

"Life defies logic. Unlike your mathematical problems." He mused aloud with a shaky smile on his face.

CHAPTER XXVI

Mrinal Chatterjee

A tall man sat in a crumpled beige shirt staring at Inspector Roy and SI Das. His black trousers were new. The inspector noticed the white tag tucked in at the last minute. The brown Ray-Ban sunglasses covered only a part of his face. His hair was ruffled and unkempt, his stubble unshaven and yet, Mrinal Chatterjee was turning heads at the police station.

Everyone – right from the constables to the petty criminals to those who had come to report crimes couldn't take their eyes off the man. He was unmistakably handsome and very tall, with a magnetic aura.

No wonder he is an actor. What else will he be?

The inspector studied him closely.

"Did Mrs Bagdi take her away?" He said in his baritone voice interrupting her silent review.

"Not yet." SI Das answered.

"Oh." He sounded expectant.

"Why not?"

"We have sent the body for an autopsy." The SI explained.

"I didn't know. I've been so occupied. My shooting schedule has been demanding and erratic. I did call Ritu but her phone was switched off. And her aunt..." He removed his sunglasses and for a moment the cops were taken aback by the intensity of his eyes. "Well, we are not on talking terms."

The inspector nodded.

"I should have come earlier." He smiled wryly.

"Now that you are here, we would like to go over a few things." She cleared her throat.

"Sure." "Where were you on the 21 November?"

"I was in Agartala wrapping up my shoot. Why?" He tilted his neck slightly.

A woman sitting on a bench nearby who had come to report about her drunken, crackpot husband hitting her for the fifth time, sighed.

"We have reason to believe that Rituparna may have been murdered on that day."

He turned his seething gaze on the inspector. She held her breath but remained calm. "Are you asking if I've murdered Ritu?" His splendidly low forehead lined into a deep frown.

The inspector let out a sharp breath. "If you haven't, then you should have no problem—"

"I was with Akshay Deb Barman. You can call and confirm."

"Who is he?"

"My director."

"We will. Ask and confirm." She let out a deep breath.

"What were you doing with your director on the 21st night?"

"I was at his home drinking. I left for Kolkata on the 22nd. Took an early morning flight."

"We will need a copy of the air tickets."

Mrinal nodded.

"How was your relationship with your ex-wife?" The SI had been weighing the actor. Looking for chinks.

"She was not my ex-wife." His eyes turned misty. "She was an irrefutable part of my life."

"You do understand that whoever killed Rituparna knew her well." The inspector spoke, her voice oddly staccato.

This charismatic man was making her nervous.

Mrinal's face froze. "Then you must catch him or her."

"Him." She corrected reluctantly returning to the cop mode.

CHAPTER XXVII

Jhorna's Dream

A wave of despair came crashing upon Jhorna. She had often imagined her mother's death but when the ailing old woman breathed her last and stared listlessly at the roof, her mouth half-open – her frail daughter shivered in desolation, finally breaking down into tears. Like a clueless infant which seeks no one but its mother.

Is God punishing me?

She mused aloud and then shuddered at the thought.

Why else will He take her away so suddenly? Is it His way of telling me that I should have never lied? I didn't lie.

She protested stifling a sob. Being silent is worse than lying. Her mind reasoned.

I am being absurd. My mother was ill for a long time. She has passed on to a better place. Her soul is in peace now.

She covered her face with her greasy palms.

It was too late to right the wrong. Too late.

Dabbing her cheeks, Jhorna went about cremating her mother's body with a little help from her friends and neighbours. She had no one else. Later, when she lay on the floor, her gaze fixed on her mother's empty bed– she thought about the old woman who had cared for her, held her and never raised her voice.

As a kid, she felt blessed to have a mother like Maa.

"Your Maa never whacks you?" The shanty girls would chorus circling around her.

"She doesn't." Jhorna would smile.

"Why not?"

"I don't know. Maybe she loves me."

"As if our mothers don't."

"Maybe she loves me more."

The girls twitched their lips in envy and hated their mothers for not being like Jhorna's Maa.

With years, the soft-spoken, industrious woman retreated into her shell. Her health deteriorating with each passing year. Finally, she took to the bed and stopped moving. Except for her visits to the squalid, ramshackle toilet. At times, she defecated and urinated on the bed. Despite all that Jhorna had endured over the years, she wanted her Maa back.

Sluggishly and agonizingly as the night aged, she realised that was not to be. In the wee hours of the morning, when she drifted to sleep, her mother paid her a visit in her dreams relaying what her conscience had told her all along.

An innocent woman was murdered and you are protecting her killer. Why?

CHAPTER XXVIII

The Clue

The SI tapped his fingers on the desk. The inspector was delayed and still not in the office. He had been asked to talk to the maid and take her testimony. Jhorna dressed in a demure grey sari appeared subdued and uncertain. She didn't want to talk to the smug, impatient khaki-clad man who was sitting in front of her. She wanted Police Didi.

"When is Didi coming?" She asked in a low voice.

The SI thought for a moment reading the tremor in her voice. "She will be here in some time. Why don't you tell me what you came here to tell?"

"Didi won't come to the station today? She squealed in disappointment.

"She will shortly. She has asked me to talk to you." He cajoled hoping what he said will serve as an assurance and make the woman spill the beans.

Her gaze strayed. When she looked back at him, she seemed more forthcoming. "That day when I went to Didi's house, I found it locked. It was after five in the evening."

"Which day?"

"The day after Didi's..." Jhorna sniffed fighting back tears. She couldn't say the word aloud.

Death.

It reminded her of the frozen stillness of Maa's shrivelled body. Her familiar, comforting smell.

The SI observed the grief-stricken woman silently. A minute passed, then another.

"I was late." Jhorna wiped her eyes with the edge of her sari.

"Didi never shouted at me for being late so I went in anyway. When I found the door locked, I called Didi on her phone. But she didn't answer—"

"Was Rituparna's phone switched off?" The SI interrupted. Jhorna bit her lower lip.

"I don't remember."

"Think hard." He prompted. "It's important."

"I don't remember if her phone rang or not." She said forcefully.

"Okay, go on. What happened next?"

"I went away and bought groceries. A few hours later, I went back to check if Didi had returned. I was about to enter through the gate holding my bag when I saw a shadow. A tall man. He didn't see me, but I saw him."

"What was he doing?"

"He was locking the door."

"Are you sure?"

"Yes."

"That man had suitcases and bags with him. I think he was there to take Didi's things away. At first, I wanted to shout. Then something about him made me stop. He didn't look like a thief. He was dressed well. Although he kept glancing to his left and right. When he started approaching the gate, I walked away."

"Will you recognise him if his picture is shown to you?"

She nodded. The SI took out a file filled with pictures of the suspects. He handed it over to Jhorna. "Take a look. You might find someone you saw that evening."

Placing the brown file on her lap, Jhorna stared at each picture carefully. Moments later, with eyes squinted in attention, she placed her sunburnt forefinger on the picture of a man. "He is the one." She whispered. Her gaze was fixed on the photograph.

"Are you sure?" The SI tried sounding casual as his heart leaped with optimism.

"This man was there at Didi's place." Her eyes lit up.

He smiled. Encouraged by his smile she went on, "One more thing, sir. There was a big car parked outside her house. I think it was that man's car."

"What kind of car? Did you notice the number?" He stared at her befuddled face and knew that he was asking for too much.

"A white car," Jhorna murmured.

"Are you sure?"

"Yes." She said with more conviction in her voice this time.

SI Das chuckled in relief. He couldn't wait to break this piece of good news to his boss.

CHAPTER XXIX

Rituparna's Diary

June, 2018

The grey stone-cut sculptures of Unakoti have a primeval air about them. I was swiftly transported to an era where time moved leisurely. The head of Gods particularly that of Lord Shiva sculpted on the primordial stones with such awe-inducing accuracy made it hard to believe that artists from another time had created this marvel.

Mrinal stood next to me narrating the folklores of Unakoti in his alluring voice but I couldn't take my eyes off the place.

"I've been told that there are waterfalls too." I ran my gaze around the steep hillocks shaded by green trees and shrubs. "I see none though."

"Maybe when the monsoon sets in, the beauty of this place will be enhanced further. Not that it is any less mesmerising now."

We continued to explore the place for a while. Walking up and down the stone staircases and paths surrounded by green.

"We never took a trip together." He reflected after a while. I shook my head.

"I am glad we came here." He took out his phone and we clicked a few pictures. After spending hours amid the stone-sculpted Gods who stared at us from all corners, we walked towards the car.

The driver was standing outside the entry gate at the parking area smoking a cigarette.

"Do you want to have lunch here? Or should we head towards the town?" He asked getting into the backseat.

"Let's eat later. I'm not hungry." We had chips and Coke in the car.

"Let's eat in Kailasahar then." He suggested.

"Or we could reach Agartala and have an early dinner."

"Fine." He said in a jocular tone.

"You look happy."

"I am happy." He winked.

It was good to see the Mrinal I had once loved.

We dined at a tiny eatery in Dhaleshwar, which served the Bengali spread. Dal, rice, fried vegetables and fish curry – the staple of every Bengali household.

When we returned home, it was almost midnight. Mrinal crashed in my place and I didn't object. I might have -- if we weren't friends but estranged spouses.

He lay on the floor on a thin bedsheet and I collapsed on the bed. The prospect of spending a night on the same bed next to him still eluded me. He noticed it too.

"You know after you left, I've been receiving countless indecent proposals." He chuckled staring at the ceiling lit in bright patches by the dim bulb.

"Good for you." I gave him a friendly smile.

He turned towards me. "You are fine with me seeing other...people?"

"Why won't I be?"

"That's not a genuine smile, Ritu."

"Give me some time."

"To do what?" He sprang up sitting cross-legged.

"To be genuinely happy for you."

"What if I don't want you to be happy for me?" He turned the light off.

The next morning we woke up to a sun-kissed room and the ear-splitting sound of the doorbell. My students had arrived and were waiting outside. Impatient and restless, they *continued ringing the bell.*

"Send them away." Mrinal said in a somnolent voice. "Let's go somewhere today. What about Neer Mahal? I'll rent a car."

"That's far away. I've school tomorrow."

"The tea plantations, then." His sleepy eyes slowly lit up in anticipation.

"What about my students?"

"Give them a break. Take an extra class some other day—"

"You are a life wrecker you know that. You ruin people's routines." I cried.

"Ritu, don't be dramatic – it doesn't suit you. Drama is for me."

A trifle ruefully, I told the entire group of ten to leave. Most of them were delighted at the prospect of a Sunday without Maths. Some shook their heads. A few shrugged. Paul, well, he grunted. While the others disappeared in minutes, he stood glaring at me.

"I am sorry, Paul. I will take a class sometime next week."

He cast a baleful look. "Is he inside?"

"I don't know what you mean." I feigned ignorance. I had never seen this side of him.

"Is your ex-husband inside your home?" He explained coldly. I nodded slightly.

"Why are you letting him back into your life?"

"We are friends now. It's different." I had no clue why I was clarifying my personal choices to my student, standing on my porch under the blazing summer sun, dressed in an old t-shirt and pyjamas.

It was my life after all. Maybe it was his cold gaze, which made me explain. There was something feral, animal-like in his stare.

"You should not let him back in. He will harm you again." He said fiercely.

Paul had hit a nerve, a nerve that still hurt from the bruises of the past.

"How do you know he hurt me? I never told—"

"Why else would you come here? Flee from your friends and family."

I was stunned by his ability to read me. Was I that transparent? "Don't worry, I will be fine," I muttered feeling exposed.

"Can I come back in the evening?" He pleaded while stepping closer. An unseen yearning peeped out of his hooded eyes.

"I am not sure, Paul. Why don't you call me in the evening? I might not be home."

"You are going out with him, aren't you?" He stepped closer.

"Go home, Paul," I said firmly turning away and without a backward glance.

CHAPTER XXX

The Breakthrough

A frisson of excitement gripped the cops who sat across each other relishing their morning cups of tea. The rays of the luminescent January sun entering through the lone window engulfed the tiny room in its warmth.

"I doubted that fellow from day one." The SI's eyes were alight.

"Don't get too excited." The inspector said in a reproachful tone.

"Why not? We have a witness and prima facie evidence implicating him."

"Proceed with caution. We don't want to make any mistakes with a man like him. If he comes to know that we are after him, he may go rogue."

The SI was bridled. He didn't like it one bit.

"Don't tell anyone else. Not even the SP. We will inform you after we are done interrogating him." She said in a grave tone after pondering for a moment quietly.

"Anything else?" He slurped the tea in one go springing to his feet.

"Nope, that would be all." She smiled sardonically.

• • •

Sunil Lahiri had not expected a call from the SI so soon in the day. That too on a busy Monday morning. Hurling expletives at the two burly poker-faced men, who stood next to each other in his cramped one-room travel agency, he picked up his phone and called his lawyer.

The phone rang a few times, but no one answered the call.

"Looks like I will have to go in alone." He cursed some more. "When you need someone, they are never there. They will come wagging their tails if you offer money. Money! That's all there is to it in this world. Nothing ever moves without it."

The burly men in white t-shirts with Lahiri Tours & Travels embossed in black on their broad chests, nodded. They always shook their heads in agreement when their boss was in a foul mood. These days they found him jittery and impatient quite often. His temper flared up at the slightest insinuation.

"Handle everything until I return from the station. I should be back in a few hours. If Malati calls, tell her that I am in a meeting. If she asks why I am not picking up my phone, tell her that I have been in meetings since morning."

"Okay, sir." The burly guy with a thick moustache replied. The other merely nodded robotically.

"Ask the driver to take leave for the rest of the day. I will call him in the evening. I'm taking the car." Lahiri said in a matter-of-fact tone.

Ambling over to the door, he sat on the stool next to it. With unsteady hands, he tied the laces of his brand new white Nike sneakers, while his mind winded back to the grilling in the interrogation room, only days ago. He didn't want to go back in. Grumbling, he walked out unwillingly, driving off in his white Scorpio.

• • •

"We meet again." SI Das exclaimed with mock delight as soon as Lahiri walked in.

Lahiri snorted eyeing the cops with derision.

"We will cut to the chase." The SI looked into Lahiri's beady eyes. A fiery sullenness had descended on the man's face.

"What were you doing at your house in Banamalipur on 22 November – a day after Rituparna Bagdi was murdered?"

He scratched his chin. Although the question did catch him by surprise, in some fuzzy part of his mind, he had expected this to happen. "What do you mean?" He hissed. Before putting his cards on the table, he had to get a fair idea of the opponent's cards.

"You were spotted by a passer-by at your Banamalipur house carrying suitcases."

"A passer-by?"

The SI glowered. "Do you want to play games, Lahiri? We don't mind. We've all day."

Lahiri's face turned grim. He breathed hard. "I had gone there to check on her. As I said earlier, she was not picking my calls."

"Why did you pack her things in suitcases and carry them along with you?" The inspector asked.

"When I found out that she was gone after calling the principal—"

"You called the principal on 25 November. The testimony that you gave earlier along with the call data that we have checked on your phone confirms that." She cut him off harshly.

Lahiri grimaced. He knew that he had been cornered. He needed his lawyer now. But the bugger wasn't picking up his calls. "I will answer all your questions in the presence of my lawyer—"

"We have an eye witness corroborating your presence at the site of murder. You were seen removing and tampering with evidence. Do you know how the court will view this?

As destruction of evidence." The inspector harangued the sullen man sitting in front of her.

His throat felt dry. Anxiety gnawed at him. "I didn't kill her. I had just gone there to collect her things—"

"You went there to remove her belongings because you knew she was dead."

"I am not a killer. I am a respectable man who runs a legit business--"

"Either you killed her or you knew who did, that's why you removed evidence of the crime." She cut his tirade coldly.

"Listen, I was not alone that evening." He sniggered waiting for the cops to pick the bait up. He waited for a beat.

"What do you mean?" The SI thundered.

"There was someone else in there. I had left my car keys inside. As I turned and stepped through the gate, I saw another man. He was lurking near the door. I think he wanted to get in."

"Who was it?"

"I don't know. A short fellow with glasses." "Looked like her kind." Lahiri scoffed.

"What kind is that?"

"Teacher. He looked like a teacher." He spelled out glancing at the inspector's inscrutable face.

She picked the brown file up, which was lying atop the old wooden table separating them from Lahiri. Plucking a picture, she held it beneath his fidgety face. "Was that him?"

"That's him."

"You do understand that if you mislead the police you will be in big trouble?" Her face was the surface of a still lake. Placid yet ready to break into ripples at the slightest instigation.

"You can rest assured, madam. I don't forget a face. Never." Lahiri asserted with fake graciousness.

"We will see. However, what you have just testified doesn't let you off the hook." The SI spoke this time.

"When you went back in – did you not bump into him?" The inspector mused aloud.

"I went back to my car and sat inside. I didn't want to step out and run the risk..." Lahiri's eyes darted from the inspector to the SI and then back to the inspector.

"Go on." She commanded.

"He stood in front of the door. Pressed the doorbell a few times. When his phone rang, he left in a hurry."

"Did he see you?"

"I tried not to be visible. I was in the car." Lahiri cleared his throat.

"There is something that has been bothering me for quite some time." She murmured. Both the SI and the suspect looked at her.

"What other things of the deceased are you hiding and why?" Inspector Roy looked straight into Lahiri's eyes.

"I-I-I—" Lahiri scratched his chin.

"I am not hiding anything. I've handed over the axe to the police too."

"Is that so?" She pursed and unpursed her lips.

"You can search my home." Lahiri challenged with an indignant look on his face.

"No." Inspector Roy continued to smile. "We would rather wait for you to hand over the evidence you have been withholding from us. Because you will."

CHAPTER XXXI

Virendra Jha

"Jha will reach in an hour. I've called and asked him to come." SI Das pulled a chair slumping down. He was puzzled by the smile that had been playing like a Mexican wave on his boss's lips since morning.

"Is there something you have discovered?" He frowned.

"We are getting closer to resolving this case, Pritam." She flipped through the other case files on her desk jauntily, content with herself. "We should be able to close this case in 2-3 weeks, max."

Pritam Das knew that his ex, never opened her mouth when in doubt. He was certain that a door that would lead to the murderer had opened in her complex yet sharp mind. "How do you know?"

"Let's just say, an arrest has a Domino Effect."

"Is Lahiri the first domino?"

"You and I are on the same page." She continued scanning and flipping pages.

"Did you go through the call lists of the suspects?"

"Mrinal made a few calls on 21 November to Rituparna which remained unanswered. Jha called her twice on 22 November. Jhorna called her once on 22 November. Dipti Patel called her several times on 22 November – again those were missed calls."

"What about Paul?" The inspector looked up. "Did I catch you by surprise? In case you are wondering if Paul has a phone, well, he does. And you should dig up his call records."

"How do you know?"

"Make a guess."

He thought for a moment. "Her diary."

"As I said we are on the same page."

"We found Lahiri's fingerprint on the axe from the fingerprint report."

"Did we find our killer?" She gave him a full, heartfelt smile. For a moment, he was dazzled.

Why doesn't she smile often?

"You think Lahiri is the killer?" He said slowly. His eyes were still on her lips which had twisted into a smile like monsoon showers on an arid desert after years.

"Let's find out." She noticed his droopy gaze and his boyish, absent-minded chuckle and forewent her smile instantly.

* * *

When Virendra Jha walked inside after parking his bike alongside several other bikes lined in front of the small and unpretentious station, his hands trembled and needles pricked his insides.

"Can I have a glass of water?" He blurted as soon as he sat on the old wooden chair facing the inspector and her deputy.

The SI went out to fetch water.

"We will not take much of your time. We have a few questions and if you answer those truthfully, you can leave in less than an hour." The inspector promised. She was feeling generous today.

Jha shook his head and rubbed his small, stodgy hands over his legs to keep them from shaking further.

"What were you doing in Rituparna's home on 22 November? On the evening of 22 November to be precise." She asked in a no-nonsense tone.

"I never went to her home—"

"You were spotted by a witness inside her home." She said flatly.

"By whom?" "Rituparna Bagdi's landlord, Sunil Lahiri."

"Wait a minute." Jha squeezed his eyes trawling his memory. She waited.

"Rituparna was absent on the 22nd. I went to check on her."

"Are you sure?"

"Yes, ma'am. It was my marriage anniversary. My wife had called several times when I was at her place. I couldn't take the call—"

"Couldn't or didn't want to?" She interrupted.

"I couldn't take the call." The teacher conceded.

"What else did you notice?"

SI Das entered the room and placed a glass of water in front of the skittish man. Jha gulped the water all at once. The SI dragged a chair from the end of the room and sitting next to the inspector collapsed a bit on it. He wanted her to lead. Interrogating Lahiri had been exhausting and it had been one long day.

"There was a car, a white car parked right outside her home. She wasn't there. She didn't even answer the door—"

"Maybe she was buried in her backyard." The SI sneered.

"I didn't know it then—"

"What else did you see?" The inspector cut in casting a disapproving look at the SI. "Go on."

"A shadow," Jha said gruffly.

"What do you mean?"

"When I turned away from the house and walked towards the gate, a tall shadow fell towards my right. Someone was there at the back of the house. I didn't want to turn back and check. Also, my wife had been calling for some time. I wanted to get out and talk to her." He breathed hard. "Can I have another glass of water—"

"I am not your waiter!" The SI grimaced.

"I will get it." The inspector stood up.

"No, I didn't mean that. I will get the whole damn jug." The SI grumbled.

"It's okay. Stay here. Talk to him." She wanted to get away from the interrogation scene. A vague idea had started to take root in the recesses of her mind and she wanted to explore it further. She was afraid if she didn't, it would just fade away into oblivion.

As she walked towards the water filter, a fair, sprightly man emerged from his cabin. "Roy."

She turned suddenly and bit her lower lip in irritation. The idea fluttered away like a frightened butterfly.

"Sir." She saluted SP Yadav.

"Do you have a minute?"

"We are in the middle of an interrogation." She retorted with a blank look.

SP Yadav suppressed a laugh. "You can say, no, Roy. You clearly don't want to be disturbed at this moment."

"We have a witness and he is revisiting his testimony—"

"Who?"

"Virendra Jha, sir."

"The dead teacher case?" She nodded.

"Strange timing. I wanted to catch up with you on that one. When can we talk?"

"Right after we wrap this up."

"Okay, walk in as soon as it's over."

"Sure, sir." The inspector stood waiting for her higher up to turn away. When the SP walked inside his room smiling to himself, she filled a paper glass with water and sipped slowly, staring at the water filter. Trying hard to recollect what she had lost abruptly – thanks to SP Yadav.

CHAPTER XXXII

Jui Roy

By the time Inspector Roy walked out of the station in an oversized navy blue thick jumper and started her red scooty, the city of Agartala had fallen partially silent. There was a dim buzz of vehicles on the road. The mist had descended and the air had turned eerily frigid.

Slicing through the chilly air on misty by-lanes wasn't new to Jui Roy, who had cycled through them in school and college. The familiar narrow lanes that winded now and then, appeared like serpents crawling their way in the murky darkness. The roads were lit only by a few temperamental street lights. Like every other evening, she had to rely on the light of her vehicle to make her way.

While her mind played the conversation with SP Yadav that she had right before departing from office.

"Media has picked up on the case, Roy. You can't blame them. Apparently, this case has everything. A young woman from a big city who chooses to live alone in a small town. Takes up a job as a teacher in a school known to one and all in Agartala. To complicate matters chooses two diametrically opposite subjects to teach simultaneously And then ends up getting murdered and buried in her backyard. " His smile bordered on a snigger.

Like all the other times, she found no reason to smile. "Is that good or bad?"

"Both. If you succeed, Tripura will know Inspector Roy. But, if you fail—"

"My defeat will be media fodder."

"Bingo, Roy." He laughed this time. "Also the CM wants me to brief him on the case."

"The Chief Minister—"

"That's what my son tells me – CM stands for Chief Minister. By the way, my son is in the first standard." He chortled adding, "All the best, Roy."

Jui moved through the roads unafraid. She had never feared the spirits, which her mother believed inhabited the darkness. Her disquietude, on the other hand, had to do more with the two-legged beasts which skulked on unsuspecting innocents like Rituparna Bagdi.

As she turned a corner and approached Saha *Kaku's* home, an old amiable man who had been their neighbour for a decade, a speeding bike emerged from nowhere like a ball of light and bumped right into her. Before she could register the shock, she had toppled and fallen on the road. Her scooty whirred like a bruised steed, a little away from her.

Giddy, she tried straightening her wobbly legs. A spurt of pain shot through her abdomen spreading rapidly to her spine and neck. Without paying much heed to the burning ache, she pulled her sweater up and tried taking the phone out. Another bout of pain made her grunt in helpless fury.

In the meantime, the biker got off his roaring bike and walked toward her. The light of the scooty fell on the man. A stout fellow in a hoodie was holding something, pointed at her.

She exhorted her mind to focus on the situation at hand. And the situation was that an unidentified man whose face was hidden by a monkey cap was pointing a pistol at her.

"Great!" She groaned in pain.

Squirming on the pavement on which she half-sat, half-lay in pain, her head reeled with the possibility to stop him from killing her and make an example of a woman who poked her nose too much. Even in her confounded state, she knew that someone wanted her out of the way and had sent his goon to finish the job.

Ducking her head, she tried reaching for the vehicle which had stopped whirring and grounded to a halt. There was nothing else she could think of defending her unguarded body with – apart from the sleek two-wheeler, which she had purchased only a year ago with her meagre savings.

Plunging towards the vehicle with all her might, she tried lugging it closer as the hooded man approached slowly. His pistol pointed at her head.

He is going to shoot me point blank with a 9 mm automatic pistol purchased illegally.

She inferred as her hands kept tugging the motionless vehicle towards her.

"How did you buy that gun? Wanted to buy one with the same make." She blurted. Her voice sounded wounded and alien even to herself.

The assailant stared at her. His eyes fixed on her stoic face. At times like these, not many made conversation with him. Most yelped and screamed in fear. Some froze like stone sculptures. Others stuttered and stammered entertaining him amply.

"Got it from Sabroom. I have a friend in the forces. Got it for a discount too." His gravelly voice was suffused with pride. His eyes glistened with the grim satisfaction of having cut a good bargain.

The inspector nodded approvingly. She had delayed her death by a few minutes. Now it seemed imminent.

"It will hurt only for a few seconds. My aim isn't rusty." He readied himself to pull the trigger. He had done it umpteen times and the prospect of killing a young cop didn't fill him with excitement or stir his conscience. It was just another job; another dreary evening about to come to an end.

Nonchalantly, like every other time he pulled the woollen cap which covered a part of his mouth a trifle lower to breathe deeply and steady himself – a trick he had mastered in the Art of Living classes taken on the insistence of his mother when a sudden loud bang threw him off guard.

It took him a moment to realise that his head had been hit by a blunt object fiercely. As the sensory receptors kicked in and blood trickled soaking his woollen cap, he collapsed on the ground in surprise and excruciating pain.

"A single blow aimed rightly can cause Epidural Hematoma in the brain. Hopefully, for this man here, it will cause death." The old man exclaimed with a smile on his face. Masterfully, swinging an old cricket bat made of Kashmiri willow wood – his one prized possession.

"Saha *Kaku!*" She mumbled. "He is unconscious."

"Definitely. If he continues to bleed, he will die in a few hours." The old man chuckled. His eyes shone in the light of the crescent moon that shone high above his bald head.

"I will call for an ambulance." Gritting her teeth, she took out her phone and dialled the number of the nearest hospital.

"Are you out of your mind? You will save the man who wants you dead?" He said bitterly.

"I need him alive." She flinched as splinters of pain darted haphazardly through her bruised body.

The old man scurried towards her. Flinging his shawl on the scooty, he helped as she scrambled to her feet.

"No, no, don't push yourself to do anything. You may have hurt your bones, hopefully not your spine." He pressed her hand gently. "I will drop you home to your mother."

"Can you do me a favour?" She winced as an excruciating wave of pain engulfed her arm. "Please look for his phone and hand it over to me. And after that--" She swallowed hard to prevent herself from shrieking in anguish. "Take me to an orthopaedic and I will be fine."

"You don't want to alarm your mother?" The old man walked over to the man lying supine on the road. Searching with alacrity, he retrieved the man's fancy smartphone in no time. But, he didn't give it to her. "Let me hold it till the medic fixes you."

Together they made their way to a popular orthopaedic who attended to patients until late in the evening. Running her through X-Ray machines, the doctor plastered her left arm and attached a sling in no time.

"You are lucky that only a bone is dislocated. You will recover in a month—"

"A month." She shrieked in alarm.

"More, if you don't rest and take the prescribed medicines." He shot back as his potbelly jiggled in support.

"I can't rest for a month." She cried in dismay.

"You are lucky that your leg and back weren't injured." He wrote a prescription in his slapdash handwriting. "Work from home." He advised dismissively.

"I am not in IT. I am a police officer. I can't work from home." She snapped back. "Is that so? I didn't notice." The doctor smirked pointing his fleshy chin at the three silver stars on her shoulders shimmering under the bright tube light.

CHAPTER XXXIII

Rituparna's Diary

July, 2018

It took me a month to fetch a pen and scribble on this notebook. Thirty days and nights of wet pillows, deep sighs, lurching stomach and blank hours that he had left in his wake. Just like last time.

That morning when Paul walked away and I sculled to the comfort of my nest, Mrinal was up and ready to go somewhere.

"I'll be back." He darted out, looking rather preoccupied and when he returned he was carrying a large big shopper filled with bottles of liquor.

I was in the kitchen making noodles for lunch. I didn't know what came over me when I caught sight of the large white bag and heard the clinking of bottles inside it.

"Get out." My words -- a hoarse whisper.

He stared in shock. His face was ashen.

"I thought we were going to the tea plantations. You asked me to send my students away."

"We will." He muttered.

"After you guzzle a few bottles."

"I just need a drink—"

"Get out of my home, Mrinal," I said with a certainty, which surprised me as well.

His face fell. "Don't do this, Ritu. You don't want to do this. You know, we have something." His stentorian voice coupled with the simmering intensity of his eyes held me in a spell.

"You destroyed it... that night." I turned my gaze away.

"I am sorry. I am more than sorry." He spoke hastily as his voice quavered. Closing the distance, he grabbed my hands. "Please."

"You will have to let go of that." I cocked my chin towards the big shopper. "It made you a molester."

He clenched his jaw. We stood still barely breathing. His phone buzzed.

"Pick up the call. Must be your drinking buddies."

He stepped back. Slowly, he removed his hands that were clasping mine and pulled his phone out from his pockets.

I wanted to say something. To rattle, hurt or simply let the steam out. Strangely enough, the countless thoughts running astray refused to transform into words. Tears filled my eyes threatening to trickle down, as he staggered towards the door carrying the big shopper.

And all I was left with was the clinking harshness of the glass bottles.

CHAPTER XXXIV

Jui & Rituparna

Jui ran her fingers over the slanted, intertwined letters penned in black with such care. Rituparna's diary was resting on her lap. Like every other night, she observed the twist and turn of the words. The ebb and flow of the Roman script that was nothing short of runes, ready to chant cryptic messages into her ears.

What did the teachers call this kind of penmanship?

Jogging her memory with glazed eyes, she slid back a bit further on her queen size wooden bed.

Cursive writing.

She said aloud without reservations in the silence of her spacious room. There were only a few days in a year when Jui Roy led her defences down. This was most certainly one of those fateful nights. Facing death in the shape of a self-important, gun-slinging, monkey-capped man who was vain enough to declare that he was a good shot was certainly not one of her glorious moments.

Conceited buffoon.

She chuckled as a sudden thought jostled her fuzzy, medicated mind.

I am getting closer to your killer, Ritu. That's why the buffoon had come to silence me.

This time she didn't contain her glee. She let it wash over her and broke down into full-throttled laughter.

"I heard someone laugh." A tall, hunched woman peeped through the door, which had been left ajar.

"Maa." She blenched in alarm. "I didn't know you were awake."

"I heard you come in. Did you eat?" Her face contorted. "What happened to you?"

"I had an accident." She lied readily. Confiding in her mother about her brush with death didn't seem like a plausible option. The woman took medication to fight depression for God's sake! "I fell off my scooty. An auto turned a corner—"

"God! These autos! Someone should cancel their licences." Her mother said crossly stepping closer. "Let me see." She leaned towards her daughter but didn't touch the bandaged arm. Jamuna Roy wasn't someone who was at ease exhibiting her concern or affection physically.

Born to a mother who expressed love through sloppy kisses on the cheeks and a father who yelled when happy, from a tender age, she had vowed to never be overly expressive. She had prided herself on her reserve and calmness. A trait her daughter had inherited as well.

"Who took you to the doctor?"

"Saha Uncle. I fell near his home." She lied. Her eyes fixed on her mother's distraught face.

"Oh. Let me heat the food. Will you be able to eat by yourself?"

"Yes, Maa. I will be out of this bandage in a few weeks. Till then, I may need to spend more time at home." She pursed her lips glaring at her bandaged arm. She hated this incapacitated low.

"It's okay to step back at times. You can't be in control always." Her mother sat next to her on the bed. She placed her thin, withered hands over her bony legs. The thick straps of her colourless sleeveless blouse hung over her hunched shoulders. Loosely wrapped in an olive green sari bestrewn with black pagoda-shaped triangles, the woman was only a relic of the beautiful woman she was many moons ago.

"It's not *okay* to lose control, Maa." Jui looked away. Her eyes were glassy with chasing the harrowing ghosts of her past.

"Your brother hung himself because he didn't want to live. It had nothing to do with anything or anyone else." Jamuna said slowly. It had taken her years to come to this realisation. Years of yoga, therapy and medication.

Jui wanted to confide about her brother – Maa's favourite child. A brilliant student who was all set to ace his higher secondary exams. The blooming pride of their family. A constant source of joy. Around her family, she often felt lost and ignored. They didn't push her away intentionally or spitefully but the shy, quiet child who was only an average student never really had much to say or contribute.

There weren't too many accolades or anecdotes in her little world. The teachers hardly showered her with platitudes and the neighbours rarely asked her for advice on how to make their children outshine academically.

Although she was in a rut socially, she didn't have an unhappy childhood until the unexpected happened. One uneventful day, her ever-smiling extrovert of a brother stopped smiling and said *no* to dinner for the first time.

She still remembers how her mother had been shocked at her son's audacity. A few days later, he stopped talking to everyone at home and locked himself in his room. Worried sick, her parents hovered outside. Coaxing, cajoling, lecturing and motivating the sullen teenage boy didn't yield any positive results.

One rainy Sunday afternoon while the family huddled in the living room watching TV mindlessly, he opened his door. Grinning widely. Hesitant at first, his parents smiled back thanking the Gods silently in their heads. Only Jui didn't smile. With a surreal smile pasted on his face, her *Dada* collapsed next to them watching a Bollywood comic caper for hours. Even laughing loudly at the inane jokes with her parents.

And all was well in the Roy household again.

A fortnight later, oddly enough, her brother lost his smile and became a recluse. Once more. Her parents attributed this to teenage trouble and rushing hormones. His mood changes continued for weeks leading to months.

One sultry evening, right after the board exams, when the entire family had gone to attend a marriage and returned late in the night sweating profusely in their grand and heavy dresses stitched of synthetic fabrics, they found his room unlocked.

Ecstatic at having finally broken the ice that had snapped the filial tie, her father tittered and her mother raised her head at the roof, thanking the magnanimous Gods. They stepped in together beaming inside-out only to discover that their beloved son had hung himself. His lifeless form dangled from the fan wrapped in his mother's mustard yellow *Kotki* sari – the one she had discarded in favour of brighter aquamarine silk to don for the wedding.

Seconds after the spotting, everything changed. Unable to take the trauma of losing a son who had been at the centre of his existence, her father passed away in a matter of months. He was a clerk in the PWD office and his meagre pension sustained the mother and daughter through school and college until Jui found a job in the Tripura police. Relieved at finding her daughter economically independent, her mother was delighted. But her happiness was short-lived.

Jui and her engineer husband whom she had met through an aunt wanted different things in life. A child was what he desired. A career in the homicide that she had envisioned since college was what she craved. It was in dealing with the dead bodies that her morbid curiosity which had nested in her since childhood could find a valid space to unfold and manifest.

And it was this inquisitiveness that made her unravel the cause of her brother's death after years of snooping around. During her years of search, not once did she think of giving up on finding the culprit behind her brother's suicide. With patience and dogged determination, she solved the gloomy puzzle.

Dada had been challenged by a boy in his class to propose to the prettiest girl in school. A girl named Sanvi from the tenth standard. He proposed to the girl to be his girlfriend at the school cafeteria. Stunned and embarrassed, she refused him instantly.

This public failure broke his spirit and to cope *Dada* resorted to taking hash occasionally with friends -- who were also his suppliers. With time, however, his smoking reached alarming limits. Although Jui's parents remained in the dark about it the whole time.

Having lost days on smoking and clamouring for a girl who had turned down the brightest boy in school without a thought, *Dada* concluded that he would never be able to reprise his position as the school topper. And after some time found the opportune moment to end his life.

The girl in question for whom her seventeen-year-old brother strangled the life out of him is single and lives in Kolkata now. Jui knows this because for years she has kept track of her. She had to.

Two years after *Dada's* death when she arrived at the truth by piecing bits and pieces of information together, she knew that there was only one person who was to be blamed for breaking her brother's heart and for ruining her family. *Sanvi.*

So she did what a thirteen-year-old would do convinced that this was the best way to exact revenge. She sneaked into Sanvi's classroom and wrote on the blackboard, a place everyone was guaranteed to notice – *Sanvi killed Ronit.* She was careful to do it during recess when the senior students were out and the class was empty.

The writing on the board created a furore. The hapless Sanvi remained absent for days. When she did return downcast and with dark circles around her doe-eyes, tongues were still wagging and the whispers hadn't died down. Even the teachers gave her the cold shoulder.

Crestfallen, Sanvi left school and town. Her frazzled parents got her admitted to a school in distant Kolkata. This sudden shift was hard on her. She couldn't fit in the new school and her grades dropped drastically.

Although she managed to pass her boards, she couldn't secure admission to a good college. This failure coupled with the trauma of a painful past caught up with her and despite being in multiple relationships with smart and eligible young men, she couldn't invest in any. After spending only a year in college, she dropped out, which sent her rolling into drugs and depression.

Jui smiled dreamily.

Her mother had returned holding a plate of food. Casting aside the remnants of a bleak past, she straightened. Deftly, her mother unfurled the daily newspaper *Dainik Shonbad* in front of her. On top of the fluttering paper, she placed the plate swiftly. The smell of rice, dal and potato fry made Jui's stomach growl. An omelette that had been rustled up hastily lay atop the mound of rice.

"Do you want ghee? The rice is hot. I've heated it in the oven."

"No, this will do." She dug in. "Thanks, Maa." She mumbled her mouth filled with food.

Jamuna's lips twisted into a sliver of a smile. She watched her daughter eat and after she was done eating, quietly walked away with the empty plate.

Once her mother was out, Jui picked her phone and called SI Das. His phone rang a couple of times before he answered in a worried tone. "What happened?"

"Can I not call unless something happens?" She stared at her bandaged hand.

"So everything is fine?" He asked dubiously.

"Go and arrest a man registered as Raghav Sen in the Ils Hospital."

"Your ex-husband?"

"He is a paid goon. He tried to shoot me but I—"

"What? Your ex tried to shoot you? Why? When?" His words came out in a huff.

"Couple of hours ago. It wasn't my ex. A hitman sent by someone who wants me dead. I've his phone. I'll bring it to the station tomorrow. We may have found a crucial piece of evidence."

She heard him gasp in exasperation. "All this happened and you are telling me now?" He bellowed.

"I had to go to the doctor to get my arm fixed."

He breathed hard again. "You broke your arm—"

"I'll be fine in a month—"

Are you okay now?"

"Yes."

"I am coming over." He said resolutely in a sombre tone.

"Listen to me. If you don't go and arrest that paid goon, we will never know who wants me dead. You do understand that this is about the investigation we are on. And the fact that we are closing in on the killer."

"I will arrest him and come home—"

"It will be too late." She protested.

"You pretend as if I've never been to your home in the middle of the night!" He said in a low voice.

"We are co-workers now, Pritam. One misstep and we will lose everything—"

"Okay, boss." He jeered.

She paused. "We have to forget our past and work as a team—"

"Fuck off, Jui." He hissed. "Don't lecture me on teamwork. I will go arrest that bastard. Next time, just don't admit an assassin under your ex-husband's name." He hung up.

If he had meant to hurt through his parting shot, then he had succeeded grandly. Jui sat and stared at the phone still clasped in her palms.

Do I still loathe him?

She wondered.

Why else would I use his name to register a man who had wanted to murder me?

Lost in thought, she unlocked her phone and typed a text to Inspector Rimbai from the Dharmanagar police station.

Hey Renzel, need a favour. Can you dig up information on a suspect?

After a minute, her phone beeped. *The buried teacher case?*

How did you know?

A few seconds elapsed. *Everyone in Tripura knows about it. All the leading newspapers have covered it. So has a local TV channel. Endless conjecture and theories going around.*

How come I've not been mobbed yet?

It will happen soon. Anyway, send me the name and will see what I can do.

Smiling, she texted back. *His name is Paul Jamatia. He used to work in a tea shop. He is eighteen now. You must look for a teenage boy who was working in a tea shop, some years ago.*

Done. Give me a week to dig into my informer network.

Still smiling, she typed, *okay.*

How are things otherwise?

Not too bad. Will catch up soon. Goodnight.

She ended the chat rather abruptly with her old friend and colleague. Typing with one hand wasn't easy. Particularly when the other was bandaged and hanging on a sling. Plus, the painkillers that she had consumed had started to kick in.

As she prepared to glide into the arms of sleep, a popular Bollywood number reverberated in the silence of her room. Alert, she tried to locate the source of the unknown ringtone. Rubbing her throbbing temple, she glanced to her sides. It took her a while to recall that she had seized the hitman's mobile and the insufferable filmy song was playing on his phone.

She found the smartphone inside her pant pocket. The call was from an unidentified number. Thinking on her feet, she decided to dodge it.

If I pick up and don't answer, the caller who in all probability is the hirer will find it fishy and conclude that the task wasn't completed.

If I let the phone ring, the hirer will be confused and his confusion will act in my favour.

Content with her line of reasoning and the split-second decision, she poured water from the steel jug into a steel tumbler. Every night her mother placed the two on her bedside table.

While she seeped water slowly, she realised that a lone painkiller will not be able to lull her to sleep tonight. Without a second thought, she popped another and waited. As the second tablet, also a potent sedative kicked in, she staggered towards the dim blue bulb in her room turning it on.

With a moony smile on her face, she did what she does every night. Grabbing a few pillows, she perched on them like a stoned queen, who was in no mood to confer with her subjects. And began reading Rituparna's diary.

CHAPTER XXXV

Rituparna's Diary

August, 2018

Trust is an invaluable gem. But mind you, when you lose it twice, it loses its charm and shine. Mrinal's departure from my life created a fanged void more potent than last time. After walking out of my home, he didn't call or text. This time he made no effort to reach out. Neither did I.

At school, I endeavoured to fill my days with work. I took as many classes as possible. Filled in for absentee teachers. Stayed after school to help the not-so-bright kids who were struggling to pass.

Thankfully around this time, a distraction came my way quite unexpectedly. I was made to supervise the Annual Day. An event, which was the pride and joy of students, teachers and parents alike. The Annual Day preparation filled my plate with much more than I could chew.

I didn't mind it one bit.

The running and yelling at school made me exhausted enough to sleep peacefully at night. Life as I knew it was moving in its usual rhythm, when on a Sunday morning after the streets were washed clean and the trees made lustrous by white sheets of torrential rain, Paul walked in alone covered in a navy blue hooded poncho.

"Where are the rest?" I asked without hiding my surprise.

"They are not coming."

"Why not?"

He whirled around waving his long thin arm at the sky.

"*But, it will stop raining soon.*" *I didn't want to teach a single student, which meant that I would have to repeat the entire session for the remaining nine learners.*

He took his phone out of his shirt pocket, ran his fingers on it for a bit, then, thrust it under my nose. I peered. Lines and lines of chat in a group named Ritu's Maths Champs spread in front of me.

I gave it a cursory read and concluded that the students had decided on giving my class a miss and gone for a stroll at the Heritage Park. A sprawling vista of green next to the Rajbhawan (or governor's residence) held in its acres of land a glimpse of the cultural heritage of the tribals and Bengalis living in this small north-eastern state. The park opened to one and all in 2012 attracting many and was a favourite haunt for all age groups.

"*Shouldn't you be with your friends?*" *I turned away from the porch annoyed at the strange behaviour of the group. I had assumed that they liked learning Maths with me.*

"*They just wanted a break. The weather is such.*" *Paul murmured as if reading my mind.*

I turned around. He stepped back. "*You should be with them. I will not be able to take an extra class. Please inform them about it.*"

"*Sure.*" *He followed as I made my way into the living room.*

"*What do you want, Paul?*" *I said without turning to face him.*

"*I want to show you...something.*"

"*What?*"

"*A painting.*"

A wave of guilt hit me for taking my anger out on a boy who had done nothing but turned up for his tuition when his peers hadn't even bothered to inform of their absence. Facing him, I smiled to convey my apology. "*What did you paint this time?*"

He held my gaze indecisively.

"Well, show me. Do you have your paintbrushes and paper?"

This time his eyes lit up and his thin lips trembled. He plonked on the armchair.

"Not so fast. You will need to remove that soaked windcheater."

Clumsily, he removed it. Water droplets trickled down forming a puddle on the tiled floor from the soaked garment. He stared at me regretfully.

"I will get the mop, you get started."

I went to the kitchen and grabbed the mop stick. As I stood there, wondering what he was doing here all by himself when his friends were cavorting in a park, he murmured: "I will do it."

"It's okay."

He stretched his arms. I handed over the stick to him.

Wiping the water off the floor deftly, like he was accustomed to doing housework, he walked past me placing the stick in its usual place. This little act of familiarity, of knowing the exact place where Jhorna kept the mop stick, at the very end of the kitchen in a corner next to the steel utensil shelf made me realise that he was an exceptional observer.

He plonked on the wiped floor in gay abandon emptying his bag of its contents. An array of pencils, brushes, paints, sharpeners and erasers splattered on the floor. Quickly arranging the things in a semi-circle around his drawing book, he commenced sketching.

I sat on the large cane armchair next to him and began reading a book named, Shakespeare and the Invention of the Human written by Harold Bloom, a man who had dedicated his life to reading, teaching and exploring the Bard of Avon. After all teaching, Shakespeare to high schoolers was no stroll in the park. It called for extensive reading and preparing over the weekends.

An hour passed. I bookmarked the weighty tome keeping it aside and gazed at his drawing book. He had sketched a rose swimming over a bed of water. "A rose?" I leaned closer to his crouched form.

He didn't reply so I went back to reading.

"Do you still see colours in numbers?" I said after a while.

"Why would I stop?"

"Are you okay...with it?"

He stopped painting "Do I have a choice?"

"It's a gift, Paul—"

"You did mention that last time." He clenched and unclenched his jaw.

"With time you will find more people like you—"

"I don't want to find anyone."

I smiled. Our gazes locked. I sprang up. "Want tea?"

He didn't respond but went back to mixing colours.

After a while, I returned holding two mugs of tea. I placed one in front of him. "Thanks." He took a large sip of the hot ginger tea.

"Tea and rains go well together."

He shook his head.

"Will you not be missed at home?" I said casually sipping tea.

"My sister will be fine. She has taken to painting. I've taught her the basics. These days, she paints for hours."

"That's lovely. How old is she?"

"She is ten-years-old."

"Does your sister study at the Rainbow School too?"

"She can't study in my school." He said with a shrug.

"Why not?"

"She has ASD."

"Autism Spectrum Disorder," I murmured. "Does she enjoy painting?"

He didn't respond for a while. "She recognises colours and likes to dabble in art." He turned around and a smile played on his lips. I returned his smile.

"Your parents must be so proud of her—"

"We don't have parents." He said simply. "We are orphans."

"Sorry to hear that."

"We have moved on." He shrugged again.

"Don't mind me asking but who pays your school and tuition fees then?"

"I don't have to pay for school. Father has waived my fees."

"Oh."

"I work part-time to meet my expenses and pay for tuition."

I was stunned. "Paul...You don't have to pay your tuition fee—"

"I don't want your pity—"

"No! I want to help—"

"I don't need your help. I can afford a thousand bucks. No big deal." He protested.

I nodded.

Another hour passed. "Should we call it a day?" I asked in a soft tone. I wanted to get started with making lunch and enjoy the rest of the Sunday, alone.

He turned around resting his gaze on me. Without a word, he began putting his things back into his bag. When he held the half-finished painting delicately in his hands, the paint on which hadn't dried yet, I said, "You can keep the painting here and finish it when you come in next."

Gently keeping it back on the floor, he zipped his bag without the painting.

"Looks like an incipient masterpiece." I smiled.

He raised his sharp chin. "What's incipient?"

"Developing into. Make a sentence with it." I said encouragingly.

He froze as if in a daze. I waited. In an unsteady voice, he said, "Are we, friends or incipient lovers?"

My heart thumped against my chest in a demented rhythm. "You are my student and I will be your teacher, always."

What had I done to make him think this way? Did I lead him on?

"Toilet?" He muttered stepping away. I could still feel his eyes on me.

"To your right," I whispered relieved to find him walking away.

Inside the toilet, I heard him splashing water in the washbasin in quick succession. Springing up from the armchair, I started pacing the room. I had to do something -- couldn't just let it be. This wasn't a boy who was prone to flirtation and flings. This boy barely spoke or opened up. His eyes, which looked straight into your soul were a leaden, sunless forest.

Dazedly, as I stood trying hard to plan my course of action despite the scrambled sense of a teacher-student relationship, his phone rang. It continued to ring as I gazed at the toilet door. After incessant ringing for what seemed like hours, I picked it off the floor and walked towards the toilet.

I stopped at the door confused.

Do I knock and hand it over? Or, do I wait for him to step out?

I held the phone closer to the door so that he would hear the sound and rush out. There was no other sound inside apart from the running tap, which was pouring water into a half-empty bucket.

As if aware of my fragmented state of mind, it stopped ringing rather suddenly. The door remained locked still. Confused, I stood staring at his smartphone when a flurry of texts hit swiftly. One of the texts read:

Where are you? We are at the park. You asked us to be there at 10 and you're missing!

(There were several emoticons and exclamation marks after missing.)

I didn't know what to make of it. It was difficult to believe that the boy who feigned innocence was responsible for sending my students away.

Why did he do that?

While I stood clasping his phone, he walked out. I raised my confounded gaze towards him. His eyes had reddened and his face was wet. "Let me grab you a towel." I returned his phone. "It rang many times."

Quickly, turning away, I crossed the living room entering the sanity of my bedroom. I let out a deep sigh and tried relaxing. Minutes later, when I walked out holding a towel, he was all set to leave. "Here."

"It's okay." He refused with a shrug. Without another word, he walked towards the door.

"Paul." I cried.

He turned.

"Don't cancel classes without telling me," I said assertively.

He held my gaze. "I wanted a moment alone. They always get in the way."

"They are my students. So are you." I tried smiling.

"I get the point you are trying so hard to make." He scoffed. "Don't worry. This will remain between us."

"There is nothing between us, Paul."

"Why? You love Mrinal—"

"It's not about him—"

"Then, what is it about?"

"I am your teacher."

He gave me a dark scowl. "So?"

"You can only be my student, Paul. Nothing more."

A strange look flashed across his face – part disappointment and part denigration.

"Do you know that all the students in the twelfth standard want to come to you for tuition? They don't want to go to Jha, the Maths teacher, but you." His mouth twitched.

"Why is that?" I was taken aback.

"I've got them convinced that you are better than Jha."

"Why would you do such a thing?" I shuddered.

"You are better than him. Your knowledge is vast and sound. You shouldn't waste your time teaching English, which can be taught by anyone. You are not meant to be an average English teacher. You told me once that this universe is a mathematical structure. Don't you see it – you are here to be the torchbearer of a subject that defines everything in this world—"

"Except love," I murmured. "Moreover, Jha Sir has a family. He needs the job. You have made a grave error. I will not be snatching away his only source of income." I said firmly.

"You are making a mistake. He doesn't deserve to be a teacher—"

"Let us not decide, who is deserving and who isn't. Don't meddle ever again, Paul." I walked past holding the door open for him to walk out.

CHAPTER XXXVI

The Morning After

"Did you scour through Rituparna's things?" Inspector Roy asked as soon as SI Das walked into her room the next morning.

He regarded her left bandaged arm briefly. "Of course." His tone reflected her nonchalance. He knew that she didn't like exchanging pleasantries or talking about her wounds, be it internal or external.

"Did you find a laptop among her things?" She kept her eyes on the files that lay open on the desk – cases of probable homicides.

"Yes."

"I thought so. Where?"

"In one of the bags. An old Lenovo, barely used. It took us some time to crack the password and to break into it. About two days ago, with the help of our in-house hacker, we succeeded."

"What did you find?" She raised her gaze but fixed in on a spot behind his frame.

"Nothing much. We went through the search history and folders. She wasn't an online person. A few emails here and a few searches there."

"What about pictures?"

"A folder named *Wedding Pics* contained about fifty odd photos of the wedding day. No other folders."

"What about her search history?"

"We've checked that too. Academic sites mostly and a few blogs on gardening."

"Gardening?"

"She may have been interested in it. We did find dried rose plants."

The inspector jogged her memory for images of withered plants but drew a blank. "Where did you spot the rose bushes?"

"In the backyard parallel to where she was buried." He said with pride. He was certain that his capable boss had missed noticing the rose bushes.

She slouched in the chair and let her mind take her to a place she hadn't been earlier. The SI pulled a chair and keeping his inquisitive eyes on his boss sat on it silently. He knew this conversation wasn't finished. Far from it.

"Did you check if the mail was sent from her laptop or her phone?" Her voice was distant and faint.

"We used a tracker to track her number and dig out all we could."

She waited for him to finish.

"Her phone was switched off on 21 November at 1 a.m. and then turned on at 2.30 a.m. on 22 November for five minutes—"

"The killer sent an email to the principal using her phone. After which he switched it off again. And in all probability disposed of it." She spoke in a faraway voice.

"Maybe. Her phone is still switched off so we haven't been able to trace it." The SI said defensively. He had tried his best to track the damn phone. A mobile phone after all is a critical piece of evidence. For crimes of passion committed due to a trigger or at the heat of the moment, chat and call histories were often enough to nail the culprit. Even in cases of premeditated, well-executed murders, the murderer often left clues in the form of an incongruous calling pattern or a stray text.

"What about Paul's phone? Did you run a check on his call list?"

"He didn't call Rituparna Bagdi on 21 or 22 November."

"Anything else?" She tilted her head focussing on him for the first time since he had sauntered in.

"The autopsy report will take another week at the least."

"Why?" Her eyebrows furrowed in annoyance.

"One of the forensic pathologists in the team is down with dengue. They can't move forward without his consent and review." He said brusquely. She was looking at him like it was his fault that the autopsy report was delayed.

"Is that all?" Her eyes strayed away from him to the door.

"Madam, tea?" An old man with white hair tamped down entered the room holding a large steel tray.

Spotted daily in his trademark black pants, an inch above his ankles and a pressed shirt that was new years ago, his face was known to one and all at the station. Only a few knew the man's name who when spoken to only flashed a toothless grin.

"You can place it here, Dipak." She beamed pulling a coaster out of her top drawer and placing it gingerly on the table. The old man nodded placing the steaming cup of tea on the rectangular, bright yellow cane coaster.

The SI stared at the smiling duo. She never smiled this freely unless she had formed a genuine attachment. He found it odd that of all people in this wretched world, she had bonded with an old toothless man who was but a nameless face to most at the station.

Once the old man had ambled out of the room holding the steel tray with cups of hot tea, SI Das remarked, "You know his name?"

"Dipak Deb Barma. He has been serving tea here for two decades." She was still smiling.

He didn't know how to reply to that. "There is one more thing."

She held his gaze.

"The man who attacked you last night is in the hospital. He is still unconscious."

"Did you arrest him?"

"About that." He paused. This was the part he had wanted to evade talking about.

"What happened?" She read the hesitation evident on his face.

"I had to report to SP Yadav about your assault to get my constables to guard the man at the Ils hospital. He is still in a comatose state and we don't know who hired him." He summed up in a solemn voice what had been brewing inside him for hours.

"You reported to the SP without my knowledge." She said with barely concealed derision.

"I called him up last night and informed him about—"

"You superseded me!"

The tremor in her voice rattled him. "He had to be informed. Your life is in danger and we need permission from the SP to dig up the hitman's call records. Don't want legal hassles. You know that--"

"Of course, I do." She cut him short curtly.

"We can't interrogate him until he regains consciousness though." He added in a tone that was midway between resentment and sarcasm.

"My neighbour hit him to save my life. Would you rather have me dead?"

"I never said that." The tenderness in his eyes didn't match the gruffness of his voice. "We need the hitman's phone to track your killer."

She placed the hitman's shiny Samsung phone of the latest make on her desk. The SI stepped forward picking it up. With a glazed look in her eyes, she murmured, "What an odd thing, this phone is. You can kill its owner, but can you really destroy a phone?"

He cleared his throat. "Go easy on the painkillers."

Before she could mouth an appropriate retort, he disappeared from the room. She stared at her desk for a while. The painkillers that she had consumed last night hadn't been washed out of her system yet. Reeling under its effect, with a peculiar lightness in her head, she dialled a number.

"Hello." A loud female voice answered after several rings.

"Dipti Patel?"

"Who's this?"

"Inspector Jui Roy. Can we talk for a moment?"

"S-ure." Came the hesitant reply.

CHAPTER XXXVII

Sunil Lahiri

He paced the white granite floor of his large bedroom frantically. It had been hours since he had jabbed his thick, long finger at his wife and son and yelled: "Don't come knocking unless it's an emergency."

They had simply stared, accustomed to his sudden bouts of madness. It wasn't the first time he had been this way – fuming and irate.

He paced some more inside his room, the door of which he had locked ensuring that no one in his family intruded and disturbed his privacy.

Agitated, he walked over to his unmade bed glaring at the scattered mobile phones.

The bloody idiot hasn't called.

He murmured as a sudden chill ran down his spine.

Has he been nabbed?

Running his gaze over the three mobile phones, he picked one up. He called a number. The phone rang and a voice answered drowsily, "What h-appened?"

"Find out if Inspector Jui Roy is dead or alive."

"Now?" The man asked groggily.

"No! After I fire a round of bullets through your brainless head!" He hissed.

"Okay, boss." The man said in a sombre tone.

"I want to know in ten minutes, clear?"

"Yes, boss."

Lahiri hung up and hurled the phone on the bed with all his might. It felt good, even if for a moment.

Ten minutes later, when his phone rang he wasn't feeling good anymore. As he stood in his bedroom in his nightclothes dialling his lawyer's number with trembling fingers fearing that the worst was about to unfold, he heard a loud knocking on the door.

"What?" He shouted.

"The police is here." He heard his wife holler in an undaunted tone.

"Why?" He yapped this time.

"They want to talk to you. Just come out and talk to them."

Does she want me to get caught? The insufferable wretch. After all that I've done for her and her brat for years.

"Are you coming or not?" She rapped the door.

He remained rooted to the floor, his eyes fixed on the window, which he had not opened since morning. He had no intention of letting the cold January air in on a day when his life was amiss. Not to mention, an open window would make him want to run for his life.

Tapping his jittery fingers on his bald pate, he stood planning as his heart thudded vehemently. Moments later, he picked up a phone that he used frequently and typed a text to his lawyer. Then, he plucked his wig out from the bottom shelf of his four-door wardrobe.

Standing in front of the large mirror fixed to a grand white dresser, he situated the wig on his head carefully, like every other day. He stared at his reflection for a moment.

His wife banged a few more times.

Grunting, he fetched a jacket and a white package that he had until now hidden with care, mooching out.

"Keep this in a safe place." He whispered to his wife as his ears buzzed. She nodded fighting the urge to fight with him for doing this to them. Her son was innocent so was she. They had never been part of his shoddy business. Their only mistake was that they had accepted his money. His dirty money had given them a luxurious life but at what cost?

At the cost of everything.

The hapless woman watched as her husband stepped out of the door. His walk was leaden with defeat. The tall khaki-clad policeman chuckled enjoying their predicament. With a wide grin, the insensitive cop instructed her distraught husband to sit in the police car. As she stood glued to the spot numbed by it all, her son appeared.

"Why are you here?" She whispered. "Go and study in your room—"

"No." He snapped, his eyes fixed on the police car. He had never snapped on his mother.

Together the mother and son walked over to the gate, observing like bystanders as the jeep cut a corner disappearing around the road.

They knew that from this moment on, their life was going to change forever. Their share of normalcy gone; their safety net ripped. The prying neighbours will know and so will everybody else. After all, everyone in Agartala knows everyone else. The bane of living in a small town.

CHAPTER XXXVIII

Tête-à-tête

"Thanks for meeting me at such short notice, Dipti." Inspector Roy smiled at the large woman dressed in a yellow salwar kameez. Her neatly pleated shiny black dupatta was pinned to her left with a safety pin. The pin had a tiny yellow duck on it imbuing its wearer with a cheerful vibe.

The inspector was dressed in a white asymmetrical top and loose black trousers. The two women looked like friends, albeit new friends. They were seated across each other in *Jhikmik,* a snug café tucked inside a patch of green, next to a placid lake in College Tilla. An area that served as the residing quarters for the staff of the longstanding and renowned academic institution, Maharaja Bir Bikram College. It was also a part not frequented by many.

"Honestly, I was curious. Your call intrigued me." Dipti smiled wanly. Her eyes were shrouded by deep circles. "What more can I tell you about Ritu?" She let out a long, tired sigh.

"I don't want to talk about Rituparna." The inspector averted her gaze.

Dipti slouched giving in to the softness of the couch. "I am relieved to hear that. I have not been able to sleep after I woke up to the news of her murde—" She left her sentence unfinished as a young couple passed by whispering and giggling without a care in the world. They walked a bit further settling on a couch.

"I want to order coffee. Do you want something?" The inspector flicked the menu off the wooden table and commenced scanning.

"I don't mind a hot cup of coffee. What else do they have? I have never been to this place." Dipti ran her eyes around the spacious café, which could do with a new coat of paint. They were seated next to a glass partition overlooking the serene lake. The sun was about to set and the surface of the lake, much like everything else was burnished in orange and red.

"They do have sandwiches and pastries." She passed the menu to Dipti.

"It's okay, I will order a chocolate truffle pastry. You can never go wrong with chocolate."

The inspector waved at the short and stout waiter with hooded eyes. He reached their table in no time. "A chocolate pastry and two cups of coffee." She ordered. The waiter nodded scuttling away.

"What is your opinion about Virendra Jha?" The inspector said in a casual tone after a while.

Dipti considered the question. "He is a stubborn and envious man. But, I think his wife pushes him to send her money all the time."

"Go on." She leaned forward slightly.

"Jha Sir's wife likes to shop, you know the usual – jewellery, saris. She is often cash-strapped. A week or so ago, PT Sir was absent. The principal had asked me to substitute for the seventh grade. 7C or was it 7 D..." Dipti clicked her tongue.

"It's okay. Continue."

"There I was standing under the blazing sun, keeping an eye. The students were playing on the football field. Another group of students was playing handball. Suddenly, I heard a man squabbling and mouthing abuses. I was surprised to find Jha Sir yelling in Bhojpuri. You see,

Bhojpuri is quite similar to Hindi and Bangla so I could make out--"

The waiter appeared holding a plastic tray filled with food and beverages. "The pastry looks good." Dipti smiled forgetting everything else.

"It does." Inspector Roy muttered glaring at the waiter and then at the steaming cup of coffee that he deftly placed under her sharp nose.

Dipti dug in immediately. Scooping a big chunk of the dark brown pastry from the pristine white saucer, she dropped it into her open mouth and closed her eyes. "Mmm... delicious." She groaned in ecstasy.

The inspector continued sipping coffee in silence. "Did you ever see Jha fighting with you know, er...Rituparna?"

Dipti dropped her spoon. It clacked on the grey tiled floor startling the couple sitting next to them.

"I am sorry." The inspector shrugged.

"No, that's okay." Dipti stopped munching reluctantly. "You are doing your job." She wiped her mouth with tissues. "If there was one person who wanted to obliterate her, it was Jha. He couldn't tolerate her. He appeared queasy and vexed in her presence. Even in the staff room, he tried to spread rumours about her."

"What kind of rumours?" The inspector took a sip of her coffee, which had turned tepid.

"You know...that she is having an affair with a student."

"I am assuming the student is Paul."

Dipti nodded.

"Was it true? The rumours."

"Of course, not. I mean she never looked at Paul that way. Although he did fancy her." She sipped her coffee. The waiter came in and placed a spoon on the table. He picked up the soiled spoon from the floor and left. Dipti dug into her pastry with vigour.

"Did she tell you anything else about Paul?"

"That boy frightens me. She had said once. But, I don't think she meant it. You know sometimes, we teachers say things when we are upset about our students – we are not serious about half of it."

"So she wasn't serious when she confided that Paul frightened her?"

Dipti gulped the portion of food in her mouth. Taking a deep breath and with a beatific smile, she said, "The *guru-shishya* relationship runs deep. It's as weighty as the parent-child relationship. What we tell those boys and girls at school touches every fibre of their body. They may appear nonchalant like they are not listening, but they do...They always do."

"Did Paul know that Rituparna was frightened of him?"

"Of course, not. Ritu was a brave girl."

Inspector Roy considered the woman sitting in front of her relishing the pastry, which had dwindled to a smidgen. For a moment she was filled with envy. Teachers impact thousands and their students in turn impact millions. She could never think of leaving such an influential legacy behind.

"Did she say anything about Jha?" She asked after Dipti was done eating.

"She wanted to mend ways with him. That's all I remember." Dipti's phone rang. She glanced at the number answering it immediately. "Excuse me." She murmured getting up and walking away.

It's her husband calling. The inspector deduced from her change in tone and need for privacy.

Left alone, she tried sipping the cold coffee. But, changed her mind once the cold liquid slashed the insides of her mouth leaving a bitter-milky aftertaste. Without further ado, she called the waiter and asked for the bill as Dipti scurried back. Slipping into the narrow space, she plonked on the couch.

"Sorry, you were saying...?"

"You were telling me about Jha and Paul."

"Yes, yes, right." She smiled. "I think I have told you everything."

The inspector thought for a moment. "Do you know anything about Paul's admission? It strikes me as odd that a boy from Dharmanagar who was never formally educated got admitted to the Rainbow School."

"He is a charity case."

"I know that. Still—"

"I think someone paid a generous donation on his behalf." Dipti's forehead creased in thought.

"Do you know who?"

She shook her head. "I don't know. You can ask Father Joseph. He will know."

The waiter arrived with a tray carrying a mouth freshener, the paper bill and a smart machine. The inspector swiped her card on the swiping machine and punched the passcode.

"Why are you paying?" Dipti cried.

"It's done. Don't worry."

"We can split the bill. Just tell me how much—"

"This is on me. Consider this as a treat from Agartala police for helping with the investigation." The inspector simpered.

CHAPTER XXXIX

Behind Bars

Sunil Lahiri lay curled in a corner. He had been huddling with his knees after being pushed into lockup. When he stepped out of his room this morning, little did he know that he would be whisked away in a jeep and shoved into police lockup.

His heart thumped in trepidation. His palms were sweaty and his eyes misty with a fear-induced haze. He had been sitting this way since he was arrested and shoved inside a tiny cell that reeked of phenyl and decomposed rodents.

After receiving a call from his distressed wife, his lawyer had arrived an hour later. The competent man had pleaded and argued using legal jargon with the inspector and the SP to no avail. His client's bail plea had been mercilessly rejected and he was retained under police custody.

"They are not going to let you out."

Lahiri sprang up and darted towards the man standing outside the cell in a white shirt and black pants carrying a brown leather bag.

"Are you getting me out?" He cried like a hopeful child. Paying no heed to the words that his lawyer had uttered.

"Listen, Sunil." The man slid his long face in between the two iron bars. The cold of the metal made him shiver. "They are accusing you on two counts. One for an attempt to murder Inspector Jui Roy. And second for murdering Rituprana Bagdi—"

"What! I didn't murder anyone." Lahiri squealed. "You have to believe me. I did not kill that woman. Why would

I kill her? Why? They can't frame me for murder without a motive. What's my motive?"

The lawyer stared at his old client. He had been aware of his shady ways of doing business, but he had never foreseen him being thrown into jail for killing a woman. Or, for sending a hitman to kill a police inspector.

"They can make you confess to murder."

Lahiri stared in horror. "They can't beat me up—"

"They can unless you cooperate." The lawyer said evenly. "You have to come clean, Sunil. Tell me everything and I will try to find a way to get you out of here." He screwed his nose in revulsion. A musty, hideous smell wafted by.

"Jhontu Malakar's calls were tracked. He received several calls from one of your numbers on the night the inspector was accosted. They are waiting to take Malakar's testimony once he regains consciousness. He was hit hard on the head by the inspector's neighbour who saved her at the opportune moment."

Lahiri recoiled in horror. He clutched the iron bars to collect himself. "If they are going to throw me in jail--" He hissed. "I bet, it won't be just me." He chuckled like a madman. His bleary eyes shot up.

The phlegmatic lawyer opened his bag and took out his notepad. He would need to take notes to prepare for the case.

CHAPTER XL

Rituparna's Diary

September, 2018

The rainbow days. When your heart expands by the little things.

You hum a tune, but the song doesn't matter. The sound of your voice, which you never liked earlier transfigures into a secret doorway to boundless joy.

I had several such rainbow days this month.

One was when a glum, rangy seventh-grader who never raised her head in the class wrote an extraordinary essay and flung her notebook at me with nonchalance. The neatly written grammatically perfect five pages about her favourite day in school wherein she used metaphors, imagery and personification was a delight to read.

The other was when a whining eighth-grader who hates poetry wrote a poem on why he hates poetry. The confident boy reasoned, "Why slice and dice", "serve uncooked rice", and turn robust sentences into "horrid blind mice." While the class laughed and I stared in disbelief at his ability to write verse effortlessly, that too with a comic touch.

Hatred is an odd force. It can make a poet out of a heretic. And a villain out of a man.

Virendra Jha's hatred towards me was palpable even in the noisy staffroom where I sat correcting and regaling in my learners' glory. And he sat fuming over the failure of his students, "who botched up even the basics."

We sat opposite each other at two ends of the long wooden table. Earlier, I found him staring at me. Noticing my every move. Ready to pounce, akin to a tiger, albeit without claws. These days, however, he keeps his gaze lowered resolutely.

Despite his odd ways, one sultry noon while everyone was sweating profusely, I decided to strike up a conversation with him. Slowly, I approached his end of the desk, next to the door. He was working on a question paper for a class test.

"Jha Sir," I said aloud.

Everyone turned to look at us.

He took a long minute to raise his head. "What?"

"Can we talk?"

"About what?"

"Can we talk in the library, please?"

He let out a long sigh. Rotated his head three-sixty degrees in a self-important manner, stood up and ambled towards the door. I followed. We made our way to the library averting the senior graders who whispered and gawked at us.

In front of the library, we bumped into Paul.

"Watch out." I cried.

Jha Sir glared. Paul returned his stare with unflinching boldness.

"May we go in, sir?" I said in a stern voice running my eyes over the two.

Jha Sir responded first by turning away and stomping into the library.

"You should be with your friends during recess." I faced Paul.

"You should be in the staff room doing what other teachers do." He hit back.

"Get out of here, Paul." I tried keeping my voice even. While he stood rooted to the spot, despite my command. Shaken, I walked away.

Inside the library, Jha Sir chose the furthest table away from the prying librarian, a middle- aged man who laughed too easily, spoke too much and wore scuffed shirts and trousers -- every day of the week.

"What do you want to talk about?" He said in a hushed tone.

Pulling a chair out, I sat next to him. "It's about the tuition classes."

"What about it?" He tightened his small jaw.

"I've no desire to steal your students. You must understand—"

"Stop interfering with my students—"

"I am not."

"You are." He hissed. "That's what you have been doing for months."

"I had started to teach because the students wanted me to."

"Which student? Paul?" He scoffed.

The way he leered made my patience snap. "If you were good enough this wouldn't have happened. They came to me because you were inadequate."

"Inadequate is the woman who can't keep her husband." His words lashed at me. My eyes welled up.

He softened his tone. "Listen, this will not end well for you. You and your radical ways of colluding humanities with science."

"I am just trying to teach."

"Is that so? Then, stop giving tuitions. Just teach English. Isn't that what you were hired for?"

I sniffled. "My students want me to teach Mathematics and I will continue to do so. Whether you like it or not."

"Again, it's only Paul who wants you to give tuitions—"

"Why would he want to do that?" I stood up. This conversation was going nowhere.

"He wants to teach me a lesson." His face contorted further. "What?"

He shrugged getting up as well. "Do me a favour." He said with a softness that made me recoil in disgust. "Tell him that Jha Sir told me about your little secret. And see how he reacts."

"What secret?"

Contented with himself, he chuckled walking blithely away. My eyes strayed from him to the librarian who gave me a toothy grin. I turned away from the man's expectant gaze wondering about the truth in Jha's words. Deeply confused with each passing second, I plodded out of the library returning to the staff room.

Right then, the recess bell rang signalling the commencement of the fifth period. Taking a quick look at my timetable, which was taped on top of the wooden desk, I began collecting the books and notebooks for class.

A shrill sound resonated in the half-empty staffroom — most of the teachers including Jha had left for their respective classes. It took me a moment to grasp that it was my phone which was ringing. Not in a mood to talk, I took the damn thing out of my bag. Mrinal's name flashed on the screen.

My head began to ache. I stood there staring as it continued to bawl.

"Pick the call up for God's sake!" A galled voice yelled.

I did as told.

CHAPTER XLI

Filling the Blanks

Inspector Roy rose from the chair stretching her arms. It had been a long, fruitful day. Sunil Lahiri had been nabbed and was languishing in the lockup. The constable manning the cell had revealed to SI Das that when Lahiri's lawyer had inquired if he had killed Rituparna Bagdi, he had hotly denied it. Instead, he had narrated his side of the story to his attentive attorney who had scribbled for hours on his notepad.

Later, the unruffled and seasoned man had been observed explaining the benefits of police confession of his own volition to avoid unnecessary custodial torture. A while later, Lahiri had willingly agreed to become a police witness and disclose details about the murderer that he had hidden from the cops earlier.

Rituparna Bagdi's autopsy report was expected to arrive in the evening. The ailing man in the core team had recovered earlier than expected and had been able to complete it in under a week.

SI Das had called up Father Joseph to find out about Paul's benefactor. The man in question had paid a large donation to the Christian Welfare Fund to get him admitted to the Rainbow School. Dipti's revelation over coffee and pastry and helped connect a critical dot.

When confronted, the principal had skirted around the topic. Father Joseph had no intention of revealing the name of the donator. He had been defensive about Paul from the very beginning and the topic of his sudden admission only made him squeamish. No self-respecting principal who had been in the business of education for years would talk about donations openly. They had a reputation to maintain.

While the principal continued to beat around the bush, the SI handed over the phone to SP Yadav who was listening to the conversation on speaker. Inspector Roy had expected the principal to not cooperate readily so she had asked her deputy to get the SP involved.

Hearing SP's no-nonsense voice, Father Joseph realised that he had hit a cul-de-sac. Within minutes, he divulged all details pertaining to the donator. The amount of money, time, date and even the mode of payment, which was unsurprisingly cash.

The benefactor's name shocked Das. Rattled, he went to the inspector to report. He found her staring at him with a twinkle in her eyes.

"You knew it." He flushed.

"I had a hunch. Is Father Joseph all right?"

"I don't think so. Honestly, I don't give a damn."

"Neither do I."

He walked towards the door. She went back to her work. Suddenly, he turned and scampered towards her. Raising his hand, he held her gaze. Popping up her eyebrows in amusement, she high-fived him with her good right hand. Together, they broke into smiles that warmed up the cold and dreary police station. Even if for a moment.

Sometime later, when the inspector's phone rang, she picked it up promptly. A dim smile played on her lips as she gazed at the number.

"Rimbai?"

"Got news for you, madam!" The inspector of Dharmanagar police station said in a mock army-jawan-like tone.

Roy chuckled. "It better be good news."

"Good or bad is for you to decide. Paul Jamatia is an orphan all right."

Inspector Roy's face fell. "And..."

"Don't lose heart. I promise the next part is good." He said in a cheerful voice. "He has a record of petty thefts in the area."

"What did he steal?"

"Food, wallets, phones. He sold the phones for a price to petty goons."

"Did he work for the goons?"

"Don't think so. He worked in a tea shop. Dealt with them only when he had a phone to sell."

"He has a sister. An autistic ten-year-old." Inspector Roy enquired.

"He has no sister. Not that I am aware of."

"Are you sure?"

"Now, now, Roy. You are doubting my informers. I may be okay with it but my fellows won't like it. They have been giving me some critical leads for years and are conceited enough to think that without them, we can't function." He laughed.

CHAPTER XLII

Sunil Lahiri's Confession

Lahiri sat facing them. His fingers drumming his legs. There was that stench again. A potent mix of urine, vomit and floor cleaner. The interrogation room hadn't changed. It was exactly the same – putrid and gloomy. But, this time he felt unusually calm. Not the least bit upset with the cops or himself.

After his lawyer had decided on their course of action, fear had left him. Rather he had willed fear goodbye. It was futile. To jump like a frightened goat whose destiny was slaughter. He inhaled. Squeezing in as much air as possible.

"Whenever you are ready." SI Das declared darting his glance from the accused to the transcriber sitting behind Lahiri. A part of her was covered in darkness. The bulbs didn't light the furthest ends of the room.

The transcriber, a middle-aged woman who had been helping the police for years now, was all set to type on her old and used laptop, a gift from her brother-in-law guarding the Indo-Bangladesh border at Dhalai. The BSF Jawan, a dedicated family man found old and new reject goods at a throwaway price and gifted them to his family members.

Ready to transcribe, she nodded slightly at the SI. "I sent Jhontu Malakar to shoot Inspector Roy. I wanted her dead." He kept his gaze lowered. He didn't want to look at the inspector who stood at one corner of the room.

"Why?" SI Das spoke again.

"I was scared." He said simply.

The cops waited.

"I was afraid that she would learn the truth."

The SI prompted. "The truth being..."

Lahiri spoke after a pause. "I was protecting someone. I don't want to protect him anymore. My lawyer has asked me not to." He rubbed his temples. "I should have known. He was trouble. Right from day one. Just, trouble. But, out of kindness, I thought of giving him a chance. Clearly, I made a mistake. A venomous snake will bite, no matter what. It doesn't care about kindness—"

"Stop speaking in riddles, Lahiri." The SI warned.

Lahiri's glare hardened. Taking another long breath, he said slowly, "Paul Jamatia. I wonder if that's his last name. He is an orphan after all. How could he have a last name?" His voice trailed off. "Did he give himself a name and a last name? When I found him, he was working in a rundown tea shop. Dirty, tattered clothes. Unwashed face. Long, black nails." Lahiri's lips twisted in disgust. "I gave him money to buy new clothes and food. He was starving, that ungrateful rascal."

"You met him at the tea shop where he worked?" Inspector Roy spoke for the first time.

Lahiri blinked as his eyes darted towards her plastered arm held in a sling. His calm shattered and his nerves tingled. "I-I may have—"

"Did you or did you not?" Her tone was ice cold.

"I did. He looked miserable, I felt pity for him. I helped him. I got him admitted to the best school in the city. Treated him like my son—"

"Why did you not mention Paul, when you were interrogated earlier?" The SI broke in.

"I didn't want him to get into all this. He should be in school. This is not the age to get muddled—"

"Where is Rituparna's phone, Lahiri?" The inspector stepped into the light. Her gaze fixed on him.

Lahiri swallowed. He knew sooner or later, it would come to this. What he didn't factor in was the inspector's razor-sharp understanding of facts. He detested this woman. And yet, he couldn't help but feel a whit of admiration for her.

"I don't have it." He avoided her scathing gaze.

"Go on, complete your testimony." She said with an unnerving sangfroid.

Lahiri shook his head. "I paid one lakh to the principal of the Rainbow School to get him admitted. He didn't want a boy from the streets in his pristine school. So much for charity!"

No one warmed up to his sarcasm. He continued disappointedly, "I provided him with everything. Paid his school fees. Took care of him, gave him a monthly allowance. How did he repay me? By killing a woman in cold blood. That snake!" He rasped.

"Why do you think Paul Jamatia killed Rituparna Bagdi?" The SI asked in a matter-of-fact tone nodding at the transcriber who raised her gaze from her laptop, giving him a silent nod. This was the cardinal part of the testimony and everyone in the room had to be on the same page.

"On 22 November, I went back to my house at Banamalipur, the one which I had rented to Rituparna Bagdi. She wasn't responding to my calls. It was around 6-7 p.m. I don't remember the exact time. It was two months ago." He stared at SI Das looking for a word of encouragement or understanding. None came.

"Why did you call her?"

"About the rental contract—"

"Cut the crap, Lahiri. It was never about the contract." The inspector stepped closer. "You do understand the meaning of becoming a witness, don't you? You must come clean. If we find you withholding information, we will have to revisit our decision and drag you to the court for murdering a teacher."

Lahiri rubbed his palms on his grimy pants, which he had been wearing for two days. "I-I-I had received a call from the principal." He said sheepishly. The inspector crossed her arms. "It was something about Paul accosting Rituparna on the Annual Day. He had heard Paul say, *don't you love me?*"

He paused. "Father was worried about his reputation. I told him to back off. The old rascal got livid. I had to make another donation of ten thousand to shut him up. Anyway, I called Paul after I was done dealing with princi. Paul dodged my calls and I didn't pursue it. I have a business to run."

SI Das snorted.

"Go on." The inspector said.

"On 22 November, I got a text from Paul. He wanted to go away to Dharmanagar. Something seemed amiss. He sounded nervous. I told him that if he went away, folks at school won't like it. He insisted. Almost begged. I found it fishy and dodged the request. Alarmed, I went over to check."

He picked up the glass of water standing on the ramshackle wooden table in front of him, drinking it in one go. "Parking my car outside her gate, I walked in. I found the lights turned off and the house eerily silent. I pressed the bell many times. Then I started to knock. I didn't want to disturb the neighbours so using a copy of the master key, I stepped inside. The house was prim. Everything was in its place. I called her name. Kept calling...don't know why...but at that point, while I was shouting, I felt someone's eyes on me. I turned and checked the porch. There was no one. I went in again and checked the toilet first. Then, every nook and corner of the house. It seemed like she had vanished. Leaving all her things behind. For a moment, I wondered if she had eloped with a man. I didn't know what to think." His head was behaving funny again. It had started to thump. He rubbed his forehead.

"What happened?" SI Das asked.

"Headache." He drawled.

"Complete your testimony, Lahiri." The inspector ordered.

"When I walked out, I heard footsteps. Following the sound, I rushed to the back and bumped into Paul. He was holding something—"

"What was it?" She interjected.

"Don't remember." He mumbled. The room had suddenly turned skittish. Lahiri covered his face with his hands. He had refused food and had been starving since morning.

"Are you okay?" The SI looked at the middle-aged man anxiously. He didn't want a critical witness to faint.

Lahiri grunted. "Paul told me that he had come to check on her because he had heard from the principal that she had resigned and left town. *I think she went back to Kolkata to be with her husband.* T-that's what he said." He wiped his tongue. Once, then a few times more. His throat felt dry. He looked up at the SI and changed his mind about asking for another glass of water.

"Go on." The SI softened his tone. "You were noticed by the maid Jhorna who has testified that she saw you carrying suitcases and walking towards your car."

"Who is Jhorna?"

"Rituparna's maid." The SI supplied.

"What was she doing there--"

"Finish. Your. Testimony. Lahiri." The inspector's voice reverberated in the room.

Lahiri blinked furtively. Inspector Roy had doubled. So had the SI. "T-that w-oman hadn't even bothered to call and inform, or pay rent. I-I c-called her number many times. But, her phone...was switched off. With nothing else to do, I a-asked Paul to h-help pack her things. While we were packing her stuff, I discovered her p-ph-o-n-e." Lahiri bit his tongue as his head swam and the room turned hazy.

"Great!" SI Das gasped as the key witness lost balance falling flat on the floor.

CHAPTER XLIII

Rituparna's Diary

October, 2018

Mrinal has a way of pushing himself back into my life. Whenever he deigns fit. This time, however, I hissed on the call:

"Don't you get it? We are divorced. I had strong reasons to leave you. One of which is you are an incorrigible alcoholic. The other, I can't mention here."

"Can you listen to me for a second?" His sonorous voice echoed. "I don't want to spend Durga puja by myself—"

"Then you shouldn't have done what you did!" I cried.

It took me a moment to realise that the line had gone silent. He had cut the call. A wave of fury washed over me. It kept bristling for a while until my students chased it away by jabbering, arguing and vying for my attention. I couldn't help it – I smiled with them while the bell rang for the final time signifying the end of another school day.

A week passed. Then another. And then it was Durga Puja. The school was closed for a week. Even Jhorna didn't turn up for work during the festive days.

As for me, I remained cooped inside my house, alone. I had never been excited about the autumnal festival that took my hometown by storm, but then, I had never been without friends or anyone by my side.

On the first day, I read. On the second, I read some more. On the third day, Dipti called and asked me to join her. I refused. I didn't want to disturb a young married couple. And I didn't want to be reminded of my failed marriage.

On the last day, when the drums in the pandals thumped nearby, I couldn't take it anymore. Draping a white cotton sari with broad red borders, I ventured out to offer floral prayers to the goddess and her heavenly sons and daughters.

After standing for hours inside a cramped pandal among a motley throng of women, who spattered vermillion at each other in gay abandon, I hired an auto-rickshaw and visited the puja pandals around the city.

The Bengalis and the tribals in Agartala, just like in Kolkata celebrated Durga Puja in all its colour and glory. Not to mention that they bid goodbye to the Goddess with a similar melancholic smile.

By the end of the tour when I walked home, the starry autumnal sky filled me with music. That night lying on my bed, I hummed Tagore's songs – those he had written and tuned as a tribute to the comely autumn.

A week later when the school reopened, I was pushed into priming everyone for the Annual Day once again. It was only weeks away and the students were loitering around in a nervous frenzy.

My days at school began with classes and ended in rehearsals at the school auditorium. Once the final bell rang and the school emptied of students, buses, teachers and support staff, I heaved my large brown jute bag filled with notebooks, books and the lunch box returning to my sanctum, which was only minutes away.

Usually, I reached home an hour before sunset when the world glistened in coral and topaz.

Yesterday, as I staggered out of school bearing the heavy bag, my phone rang. I ignored the rings. While opening the rusty gate, my gaze darted towards the porch. And I froze. There he was, leaning against the vapid wall of my porch. His white kurta cast a hallo around him. His penetrating eyes fixed on me.

He smiled, the way he does whenever he is with me – all soul, no vice. This time, however, I didn't warm up to him. Every step that brought us closer irked me. The anger returned.

"What are you doing here?" I yelled as a bike sped by on the road behind us.

"I have a shoot again—"

"I don't care if you have a shoot or not. You can't keep coming here. I want you gone. Gone!" I flung my bag on the porch. "Get out, Mrinal."

He stepped closer. I stood rooted to the spot. A sudden gush of fear encompassed me. I couldn't raise my gaze. My heart drummed. I dug my nails into my palms.

"I am not going to touch you unless you want it. Ever. Again." He whispered standing only inches away. "I made a mistake. A grave, unpardonable error. It won't happen again, Ritu."

Soothed by his words, I breathed. I realised I had caked the air inside my lungs.

Listlessly, I stepped towards the door. He raised my bag off the floor. "Are the keys in your purse?" He said in a low voice.

I must have nodded because I found him running his long fingers through my things and growing impatient every second.

"Just give me the bag," I whispered.

"No." He snapped.

After minutes of search, he fished the keychain out. "We bought this at Esplanade." He murmured as I unlocked the door stepping inside.

"You didn't want to. I had to insist."

"You said you had fallen in love with the child Krishna carved in wood." He chuckled.

"I had." I dropped my bag on the armchair. "You've to stop this. This is not right. I have to move on. So do you—"

"What if I don't want to?" The question sounded like a plea. "We can remarry."

"Why would I want to do that?"

"We can get married in court and live here. Away from everyone else, just you and me."

"You mean you, me and your bottles of alcohol."

"You will have to give me some time to change—"

"You can't change, Mrinal. I mean this is not how you beat addiction. You need to check into a rehab. More than love and companionship, you need medication and help from the experts."

"I will do that too if you promise that you will consider my proposal."

"No, no. Don't look at me like that?" I smiled wryly.

"Like what?"

"Like it's going to be different this time."

"Well, all I can say is that you should find out."

"I am going to make tea, want some?" I walked towards the kitchen avoiding his seething gaze. And his promising plans.

"Ritu?" He stood blocking my path. "I am making money now. I've got a few offers from TV as well. If it's about money—"

"Don't insult me, please." I tried slipping past, he grabbed my hand. Without another word, he pulled me into his embrace. This time my body didn't want to jerk free. I heard him sigh. So did I. We stood holding each other for what seemed like an eternity.

Mrinal left before midnight. His slack-jawed friend picked him up. I had to finish checking notebooks and prepare for class. After hours of back-breaking work, sleep washed over me. Before I knew it, the bright morning light flooded in heralding the beginning of a new day.

It was an important day. The Annual Day of the Rainbow School was the biggest event on the calendar. A make-or-break affair for the school. Students were scrambling around excitedly. Trying on costumes. Chatting. Giggling. Whispering.

Teachers were busy supervising, at times yelling in horror at slip-ups. I kept moving from one end to the other, checking, explaining, instructing and smoothening the edges. Rounding it all up. Making everything and everyone stage-ready for the big performance.

As I walked past the principal's room I noticed a shy, wispy girl standing with her shoulders hunched, her head bowed and her face downcast. I peered into the principal's room. Father Joseph wasn't inside. Curious, I asked the girl, "What are you doing here?"

*"I was asked to wait here. I was found in the **green corner**."*

*Located at the furthest corner of the school, next to the football and basketball fields, the **green corner** was a patch of green shaded by several mango and jackfruit trees. An isolated area where the students were forbidden to set foot.*

"What were you doing there?"

"Dancing."

"You were practicing for the event?" I asked gently.

"No." Pat came the reply.

"What do you mean?"

"I'm not participating in the event."

"Why not?"

"I don't like to dance--"

"Then why were you dancing--"

"I love to dance. Not in front of people but around trees. By myself."

I was intrigued. "Why?"

"*Makes me happy.*" *She said simply.*

"*Okay. Go back to your class.*" *I smiled.*

"*But, I was punished—*"

"*Not anymore. Go before anyone catches us here.*"

Smiling impishly, she hopped a bit, then stood upright scurrying away. While I was left to wonder if dancing for joy was any less than the high of performing for an audience.

In the evening, when the auditorium filled up with parents of all shapes, sizes and temperaments, students made their way to the stage in groups. Each group was in a different colour. Hues of sunset and sunrise. Of oceans and skies. Of flower beds and woods. Working in harmony.

Each group was led by a teacher-in-charge whose garment matched the performers' costume. Once the last group went on stage, a surge of relief swept over my exhausted body. Stepping out of the green room, I stood leaning against the wall. My mind blank. My limbs jelly.

"*Tired?*"

I jumped.

"*Paul? What are you doing here? You should be at the entry gate—*"

"*Everyone has entered.*"

"*Go back. You shouldn't be here.*"

"*Why not? Does my presence bother you?*" *His gaze shattered my moment of peace.*

"*Where are your friends—*"

"*I don't have any friends.*" *He cut me off.*

"*You should make friends. Loneliness is a jailhouse.*"

"*Says the woman who chose to stay alone, away from her people in an unknown place.*" *He smiled faintly.*

"*I never knew you can talk this much.* "*I murmured.*

"*You don't know a lot about me.*"

"What if I told you that I know your l-ittle s-secret?" I was not good at lying but this appeared to be the right moment to ask what Jha had incited me to.

His jaw hardened. "What secret?"

"I came to learn about your secret—"

"From whom?" He hissed.

"How does it matter? I just did."

"It does matter." He stepped closer.

I turned. He grabbed my hand, "Don't you love me?"

"No. You must accept this--"

"Why not?"

"You are my student—"

"Stop the bullshit. Do you love that ex-husband of yours?"

"Maybe, I do." I bit my lower lip. He loosened his grip but stood still. I could smell his ragged breath on me. "I love you." His voice, a solitary leaf quaking on a tree branch in the middle of a storm.

I didn't know what to say. There was nothing left to say.

Strangely after that evening, everything went back to normal. A sunlit, sanguine morning after a dark tempest.

Paul was his usual self. Silent but attentive. Taciturn and condescending, but brilliant.

Last Sunday, when the students were gathering their things and packing their bags, Paul showed no sign of leaving with his peers. I was glad he didn't. Since the time Jha had told me about his secret, I've not been in peace.

What was Paul hiding and how did Jha know about it?

When all was clear, Paul locked his gaze with me. It was the signal I needed.

"I want to ask—"

"I know. Before I tell you about it, I want to show you something." He said unzipping his bag that he had zipped minutes ago before his friends. With light fingers, he took out a rectangular object wrapped in an old newspaper.

"This is for you." He looked at me with expectant eyes.

I beamed. The Annual Day scuffle seemed like water under the bridge. Hurriedly, I tore away the newspaper and found the painting he had been working on.

"When did you take it away?"

"Two weeks ago."

"I didn't notice. The red of the rose is so bright..." I looked closer. "Although the petals are bleeding in the aquamarine water."

I lifted my head. He was scrutinising me. "You don't know my secret do you?"

"I-I-I..." My tongue felt heavy. My breath juddered out.

"Let me tell you then." He came closer.

The house is empty. The roads are silent. Barring the passing of an occasional vehicle. Everything around me is cold and distant. I grip the edge of the t-shirt I am in. The room whirls. A scream undulates in my chest and erupts as a strangled squeal.

CHAPTER XLIV

Getting Closer

Pritam Das is never late to the office. Today, however, he is an hour late and has no qualms about it. He has got the news that will make his boss more than happy. Precisely why he took his time under the shower humming innumerable rock-solid Kishore Kumar numbers in his off-key voice.

A good thirty minutes later, after stepping out of the shower, instead of running through his calls and texts, he lounged on his father's easy chair digging through *luchi* and *begun bhaja,* the special breakfast served in the Das household only on Sundays.

His perceptive mother kneaded, rolled and fried the *luchi* and *bhaja* deftly in under thirty minutes when she found him singing in the shower. She wasn't informed about his time of departure. She guessed it by the mood he was in. And had instantly decided to turn a Wednesday into a Sunday.

A bevy of mothers can make for a competent team of investigators. Any day.

He thought fondly of his round and smiling mother who doted on her only child like no other. Picking up his pace a little, he walked through the familiar corridor of the police station making his way to his boss's room.

"You are late, Das." She didn't lift her eyes from the file she was scanning with hawk-like focus. Instead of the blue sling, her left arm was tied to a pink sling.

"Nice sling." He dragged out a chair sitting opposite her old wooden desk. It was just another day at work. Although he would have liked it to be different.

"I've been waiting to share the details of the autopsy report since it came in an hour ago." She raised her gaze focussing on him.

"I've got news—"

"Can you get the file from the cabinet?" She pointed her chin towards the gunmetal grey filing cabinet on her left. Pulling his chair out, the SI sauntered towards it.

"It's in the first—"

"Found it." He said opening the report and running his eyes over the pages. After minutes, he uttered three words aloud, "Edema. Traumatic asphyxia."

"Right. This means she hit her head, we still don't know, how. And died later due to a lack of oxygen flowing to her lungs. Such deaths occur in excavation sites, where workmen get buried and are unable to escape the sudden overlay of sand or soil."

SI Das gasped in horror. "Was she buried alive?"

She continued to speak like he hadn't spoken. "We have noticed earlier that her finger and toenails were missing so she may have tried to claw her way out. Only she didn't succeed."

The SI listened unable to make sense of what he had discovered.

With a dreamy look in her eyes, she continued. "She lost consciousness due to a skull injury as it happens in cases of Edema patients. Later, she was dragged out of the house and buried at the back in a two feet deep pit, which was meticulously covered up."

He placed the report on her desk. "We went through the CCTV footage of the camera installed outside Father Joseph's room. On 1 November 2018, which was a Thursday, Rituparna was seen entering his room. She was in his room for forty minutes. When she came out, she looked upset." "What about the entry-exit gate camera?"

"Teachers, students, staff going in, coming out. Noted Rituparna's entry-exit pattern too. Nothing remarkable, odd, or suspicious in the recordings."

"Hmm."

"The hitman Jhontu Malakar is up on his feet. He has recovered well at the hospital and is ready to be thrown into the lockup." He smirked.

"Take his testimony. It will help us frame Lahiri and keep him in check."

"Consider it done." He grinned this time.

"What about Rituparna's phone? Lahiri mentioned in his testimony that he has it—"

"Providence. Sheer luck." The SI cried in excitement.

"Gaffe, I would say. He had no intention of telling us that. Paul after all is his foster child. And he is his godfather. I wonder if it was altruism that made him adopt Paul or something else."

"The only way to find out is to ask Paul." SI Das replied confidently.

"Where is he?"

"In the interrogation room. Waiting. He wants to talk to *you*."

The inspector narrowed her eyes in thought. A moment later, she picked up her phone and rose up. Okay. Let's go then. I wonder how Father Joseph is taking it. A twelfth grader getting arrested for the murder of his teacher."

"Not just any other student. But, the one he admitted after accepting a hefty donation."

"We'll need to catch up with him on the discussion he had with Rituparna on 1 November."

"He may say it was an academic discussion."

"Not *might,* he *will.* You must ignore what he says and dig deeper."

The SI nodded in acknowledgement.

"Why don't you go to the Rainbow School and find out and I'll handle Paul?" "It's Paul then?"

"Well, Mrinal has a solid alibi. He was with his director friend Akshay Deb Barman that night."

"I did follow up on that. He wasn't lying. There are calls and texts to prove that they had met up that evening and he had spent the night there. He left for Kolkata in the morning."

"And Jha?" The inspector asked with a light in her eyes. SI Das knew what that look meant. Jui Roy relished putting people on the spot and dissecting their theories in her head. What she loved most was to refute the dumb deductions and present her version with an air of superiority and a half-smile.

The SI averted her gaze. She was trying to read his mind like she always did. "He was in his room all right. The CCTV footage from the entry-exit gates confirms his innocence. He didn't step out of the campus that day."

"But, he did on 22 November. He wasn't lying when he said that he had gone to check on Rituparna. He couldn't be sure that the woman he hated with all his life had left town. He must have felt empty – there was no one to detest now."

The SI grimaced. "I wanted him to be the one. He does look the part."

"Come on, Das. You're above that. And if it's any consolation, he did play a part. He did."

"What part?" The SI's eyes widened.

"We'll come to that. Don't forget to give Jha some credit. After all, it was he who told us about Paul hiding in the shadows at the site of murder on 22 November."

"Paul was found at the scene? --"

"Not on the 21ˢᵗ but 22ⁿᵈ, as corroborated by Virendra Jha. Remember, he mentioned a *tall shadow*?" She interjected.

"We still need Paul to confess." He countered.

"That we do." She walked towards the door. "What about Rituparna's phone? When will we find it?"

"Ma'am." Constable Chakma cleared his throat. When he noticed the SI, he blurted deferentially, "Sir."

SI Das smiled beatifically conveying that he was above such petty notions such as governmental hierarchies and the need for lower ups to salute and respect the higher-ups.

"Ma'am, Mrs Lahiri is here. She has a package that she wants to hand over."

"Okay, I'm heading to the interrogation room. She can give it to SI—"

"No, Ma'am. She wants to give it *only* to you." The constable evaded looking at his boss.

"Okay, let's meet Mrs Lahiri, then." She smiled at the SI warmly, who had lost his yogic smile and was now sporting a frown on his forehead.

Together they walked through the corridor, which ran adjacent to the small rooms housing cops, petty criminals and the administrative staff. To their right in the waiting room, which was meant for visitors, an unsmiling woman with large, dispirited eyes sat crouched on the chair. As soon as she noticed the khaki-clad inspector entering the room, she cried,

"Madam."

Inspector Roy asked the men to wait. "I will talk to her alone."

The SI shrugged. Constable Chakma sighed.

"What?" The SI glowered.

"Nothing, sir."

"Why did you sigh?"

"I'm doing yoga these days." He lied promptly.

"Oh, good." The SI looked away unconvinced with his subordinate's answer.

Inspector Roy dragged a chair as the SI and the constable squirmed. It was a strange dilemma akin to the Shakespearean, to be or not to be. To be a gentleman and help the woman or to let her be.

Unaware of the thoughts that ran through her colleagues' minds, she placed the chair closer to the nervous woman and said gently, "Please, sit down. You wanted to meet me."

"Madam." Slowly, she took out a white envelope from her brown leather bag. The very envelope that her husband had handed for safekeeping before he was arrested. "He asked me to give it to you. There is a phone inside." She paused.

The inspector accepted the package from the hesitant woman and waited. She knew Mrs Lahiri was weighing her options and fighting an internal struggle at this moment.

She is here to confide in me about something.

"Thank you. Is there anything else?"

The distressed woman rested her gaze on her hands that she had been wringing constantly.

The inspector continued smiling encouragingly. "Mrs Lahiri, we never mention our source of information. In the state of Tripura, we have a large network of informers who work for us. Their identities are never revealed. No one knows who they are and we pretend we dug out all the clues by ourselves."

"He had an affair. Sunil...years ago. I had met her once in Dharmanagar. A widow. She was..." She raised her gaze.

Her eyes had turned moistened. "Beautiful. Unlike me. I think he wanted to marry her. I don't know if he did. I confronted him about her. He said it's none of my business." Tears rolled down her cheeks. She sniffled a few times.

"I wanted to walk out. Give him a divorce. But my parents intervened. They made him swear that he would take care of me and my son. They didn't let me leave him." She unzipped her bag taking a clean and pressed white hankie out. Wiping her eyes and nose with it she continued, "Last year, she died. In a house fire. I think it was gas leakage. They had a daughter...together."

Inspector Roy listened carefully with glassy eyes. Nodding only when the woman needed a show of support to keep talking.

"What happened to the daughter?" She asked in a detached tone.

"I've heard she is here in Agartala. I don't know where he has hidden her. Can you help me find her?"

"Why?"

"It's not her fault that she was orphaned. Or born. Now that he is in jail, I don't want her to be left alone. A young girl all by herself. It's not safe."

Inspector Roy smiled at the goodhearted woman. Despite her nerve-wracking experience with the dregs of society, for a flickering moment, her belief in humanity was restored. As she ruminated on the startling goodness of Sunil Lahiri's wife, her phone trilled. Frowning, she squinted her eyes at the number. The name on the mobile screen turned her frown into a smile.

"Rimbai? What timing? I was thinking about you—"

"Oho! Why, why? May I know to what I owe this good fortune? I hope it's not related to the murder."

"Actually, it is."

"Breaks my heart!" He mocked in his loud, fat, warm voice. "Okay, let me first brief you on what I've uncovered. You see, I don't like to be told that I'm not thorough—"

"I had never said anything like that."

"Well, your tone did imply it. Anyway, I'm pulling your leg, Roy, so relax."

Inspector Roy remained silent.

"I found out a few things that might be of help to the case. Although I must warn you it may not make much sense at this point." Rimbai boomed.

"Tell me."

"Sunil Lahiri was often seen with a woman named Charu Deb. A young widow. I don't know if they tied the knot. But, they did sire a daughter. The daughter wasn't normal—"

"What do you mean?"

"She is what they call—"

"Autistic." Inspector Roy completed her sentence in a whisper. She didn't want to alarm Mrs Lahiri who was wiping her eyes still.

"How did you guess?"

"Long story, Rimbai. Anything else?"

"No, that's all I've got."

"Good. I've to go. Thanks." She cut the call before he could extend the conversation.

"We will find out about the girl soon, Mrs Lahiri." Inspector Roy promised before heading out of the room.

SI Das and constable Chakma followed.

"Call Mrs Bagdi and hand over the body to her and all the things of the deceased—"

"What about the diary?"

"She can have a copy of it if she pleases. But, I want to give it to someone else." Inspector Roy declared with a cryptic look on her face.

"Okay, I will do that after I've a talk with Father Joseph." The SI scuttled out of the station. Kick-starting his bike, he dwelt on what Jui had said about the diary.

Jui and her mysterious ways.

He sniggered hitting the road.

CHAPTER XLV

The Confession

"How are you?" Inspector Roy said perfunctorily sitting across the rangy boy who was still wearing his school uniform. Pristine white shirt and azure blue pants.

"SI Das arrested me at school like a fugitive. He couldn't wait till the last period. I was summoned from class and asked to get into an old noisy jeep parked outside the school gate. Father Joseph didn't even come out of his room. That moron assistant of his, Pintso Bhutia walked me out." He rambled with a poker face.

"I am sure not many saw you get inside the *old* jeep. Sorry, we couldn't get you a Merc!"

He shrugged. "But, they spotted me being called out."

"Too bad your reputation was tarnished."

"What does that SI think of himself? He told me that he is not handcuffing me because I was still in school. What that idiot doesn't know is that he can't arrest me until I turn violent?" He scoffed condescendingly.

"Well, you're lucky we're going by the law books. Most cops I know, don't."

"You think you know it all, don't you?"

"We're not the ones who murdered our teacher and buried her, so do forgive us, if we come across as vain."

Paul glared. His face hardened.

"You wanted to talk to me?" She gave him an unblinking stare.

His eyes simmered. "Yes." He snarled. "I want to tell you the truth."

"I am all ears." She smiled faintly.

His face changed from being impassive to that of a passionate lover. "I loved Rituparna Bagdi. I was the one who made everyone see the genius in her. It was me. All along. I had convinced everyone in the class to go take Maths tuitions from her. I did so much for her. I had even dedicated a painting."

"I thought you painted because you interpreted numbers and text in colours."

He stared at her incredulously. "How do you know?"

"Rituparna mentioned it in her diary. She also mentioned a painting that you gifted her. I didn't find that painting when we looked through her things. Where is it? The one with a bleeding rose."

His eyes lit up. "I didn't know that she had a diary. What else did she write—"

"Where is the painting, Paul?"

"I took it away."

"We'll need that painting back—"

"Why?" He hissed.

"I'm sorry if it's of sentimental value but for us, it's a piece of evidence—"

"For doing what?"

"For validating your claim that you loved her." She said in an assuring manner.

Paul considered her words. Slowly, the harshness of his glare was replaced with an odd softness. Like she had finally comprehended what he had been desperately trying to convey.

"The painting is in my home. Inside the steel almirah. You will find the keys atop it."

"Okay." She knew he was speaking the truth.

He smiled. "You know that's why I wanted to speak to you. I knew you would get it. Not everyone understands the enormity of love. The all-encompassing nature of it. It's a living, breathing force. Not an apparition."

"I'm sure it is—"

"It is. You know -- it is. You have experienced it too." He smiled tantalisingly.

She felt a tightness in her chest. "What do you mean?"

"Your brother killed himself because he couldn't take it too."

She held her breath. A clock started ticking in her head. "You've done your research."

"I have. Do you want to know what else I've found out? Your brother was doing drugs. You saw it. His days of laughter and non-stop banter. Followed by days of silence and isolation. Your parents didn't. But, you failed to save him. You were naïve then, too naïve for your own good." He chuckled victoriously.

Inspector Roy had tackled hardened criminals, but she had never been cornered during an interrogation. For the first time in service, her nerves jangled. That too in front of an eighteen-year-old schoolboy.

"How did you find out about my brother?" She heard herself whisper.

"Never mind. Let's just say, I've my sources just like you do."

"You seem to be quite resourceful." She cleared her throat. "Although I must tell you that my brother didn't die at the altar of love. He died because he wasn't ready to come second. A coward, some may say." She contorted her lips into a smile.

He clenched and unclenched his jaw.

When she saw that her remark had made the desirable impact, she continued, "I wonder why a bright, resourceful boy like you would want to murder his teacher--"

"I wanted her to love me back. She didn't. She wanted to go back to that weakling, Mrinal. I tried convincing her. She didn't listen. I had to kill her. How else would our love be preserved? I had to immortalise our bond."

"Poetic." The inspector said with a deadpan face. "Let's start at the beginning. Shall we?"

Paul regarded her, trying to detect a trace of sarcasm or distrust. He didn't find any. Slowly, his face relaxed and he began, "I wanted to speak to her. I needed to speak to her. To hear her voice. She had been avoiding me at school. I wanted things to be normal between us. She dodged my signals. Evaded talking to me. I couldn't take it any longer. I went to her home and pressed the bell—"

"When and what time was it?" The inspector intercepted.

"21 November around 9-9.30 p.m. She opened the door after I had stopped pressing the bell and started yelling her name in despair. She didn't want to talk to me. She wanted me to leave. I didn't. We got into an argument. I wanted her to honour our love—"

"You mean she loved you too?"

"Of course."

"What made you think that she loved you?"

"We had such intense discussions on mathematicians and mathematical puzzles. At times, we sat in silence for hours. I would solve sums, and paint. She would read a book and cook. There was a bond that couldn't be defined by the boundaries of this world." He said with love in his eyes.

"Touching." The inspector said evenly.

He paused waiting for her to speak again. When she didn't, he continued, "I wanted her to promise that she will steer clear of her husband. I was ready to wait. We could work this out. It was only a matter of time until I earned enough—"

"Earn? You are in school, supported by your foster father who paid a hefty donation to get you in—"

"I aced the admission test. Ask Father Joseph. Still, he asked for a donation." He twisted his face in disdain.

"Maybe because you had no formal education. Not to forget that you are an orphan."

His eyes glistened with fury. "I am an orphan but that's not my fault."

The inspector was bridled. "I didn't mean to—"

"I know." He cut her off. "I was not dependent on anyone. Unlike the rich kids, I was earning my living in Dharmanagar."

"You were working in a tea shop."

"I had to." He riled up.

She backtracked once again. "I understand. There is no shame in work. Work is worship."

Paul chuckled. "You've done enough damage control for a day."

She held his gaze. For a young boy who had been charged with murder, he was incredibly calm and spunky. And yet, there was something about the boy...that worried her.

"Go on, complete your story."

"It's not a story. It's the truth."

She nodded.

"We got into an argument. It was always about the same thing. My unconditional love versus her denial. She didn't want to acknowledge her feelings for me. While arguing, a moment came when we both realised that words were not enough." He smiled fondly at the memory.

His gaze lowered. "We hugged. Holding her close, I whispered in her ears that we were meant to be together.

Suddenly, she pushed me away. I stepped closer and then…" He wiped his lower lip with his tongue. "I don't know what happened then. She lost balance and fell."

"Lost balance? You didn't push her?"

"I may have. I don't remember." He slouched on the chair.

"What happened next?"

"I felt her pulse. There was none. I didn't know what to do. I panicked. Then, I noticed the axe in the living room. Turning all the lights off, I walked out. Under the moonlight, I dug for hours. Finally, when the grave was ready, I carried her in my arms and gently placed her over a bed of soil. Her lovely face was serene and at peace. I kissed her for the first and last time. With a shattered heart, I buried her."

"Sounds perfect. Except for the fact that Rituparna was alive when you buried her."

His jaw dropped. "What?"

The inspector remained silent. She knew he had heard him.

"This can't be true."

Her eyes glimmered. "Did you send the resignation email to the principal?"

He shrugged. "Had to convince the daft buffoon that she had got bored of working in his silly school."

"This is your opinion about your principal and your school?"

"Precisely. I've many other thoughts on my beloved school, should I share them—"

"Why did you send the email at 2.30 a.m.?" She whipped.

"Her phone had died. I charged it and sent it later at night." He explained in a clinical tone.

"In her diary, Rituparna mentions a secret that you shared, which frightened her terribly. What was it?"

"Oh, no! The damn diary, again."

She gave a curt nod. "What was the secret, Paul?"

"Lahiri is no Samaritan. He got me admitted into the Rainbow School to cover his dirty secret. He has an illegitimate daughter, the one he dumped on me to fend for."

"The autistic sister of yours is his daughter?"

"She is his daughter, all right. But, not my sister." He hissed.

"You didn't like looking after her—"

"Why would I like that?"

"One of your friends heard you talking on the phone to Lahiri." She improvised. "He said you sounded upset and asked him to get someone else to look after her."

"Maybe. I was done looking after her!"

The inspector crossed her arms reflecting on what Paul had confessed. He waited for her to turn on him again.

"We are done, I believe." Her eyes darted back focusing on him.

"Great." He said conciliatorily.

"There is just one thing that confuses me." She raised her chin pensively. "Why did you not defend yourself? You could have denied committing the crime. You could have blamed someone else. Why didn't you?"

He smiled like he was waiting for this question. "I love Rituparna and I won't dishonour our love by lying and playing games."

"Sounds romantic but strange—"

"Strange?"

"A mathematical mind is usually calculative, not impulsive. There is something you are not telling me—"

"I've told you everything."

"Well, I hope you are not lying." The inspector grumbled walking out of the mildewed room.

CHAPTER XLVI

Misty Days

A day after Paul confessed to murdering his favourite teacher and the love of his life, the city of Agartala was enveloped in a thick, grey mist that hovered over the narrow serpentine lanes and the arterial roads. People covered themselves in woollens from head to toe, vehicles had to turn their lights on so as not to bump into each other and the strays looked for corners to snuggle in the cold.

Winter was on its way out. The silvery smoky coldness that floated above the tall buildings was but a glimpse of its receding form. A haze before the spring sun blazed and warmed the small town again.

At the West Agartala police station, Inspector Roy and her SI discussed the case, which in the media had created an uproar as the *Dead Teacher* case. Deprived of eyeball-grabbing news stories for months, the local media was having a field day.

Painting it as a *crime of passion,* a student's unrequited love for his teacher, every leading Bangla newspaper, be it *Dainik Sambad* or *Syandhan* had made Paul Jamatia, a household name. A misunderstood, brooding anti-hero. A lover who was pushed to commit a crime due to his teacher's indifference and betrayal.

Strangely, Rituparna the victim who had been buried alive was being portrayed as a woman of dubious character. A teacher lacking morals. A divorcee who was hobnobbing with her student and ex-husband at the same time. An allurer of younger and older men. A witch.

"Her reputation is being butchered." The SI dropped a bunch of Bangla newspapers on the inspector's desk.

She clutched the desk with her good hand. "Isn't it always? A woman is declared guilty even before a crime is committed."

"Here at least a crime was committed." The SI sneered. "The bad part is that the criminal is being touted as the hero. And the good part is that you have become a celebrity—"

"That's the last thing I want. Fame at the cost of a murdered woman who can't defend herself." She hardened her stare. "What did Father Joseph say?"

"He denied."

"And you did nothing to get the man to speak--"

"I've tried. He kept on saying that she was in his room to give a detailed report on the Annual Day. Budget, spend and the like--"

"Which only means that he is hiding something."

"Could be."

"What about Rituparna's phone?"

"We've found calls and impassioned texts from Paul but nothing on 21 or 22 November. In fact, he had stopped calling and texting her a week earlier. I've mailed you the transcripts of the texts."

"When did you send?"

"Hours ago." The SI said smugly. He was expecting a pat on his shoulder for his thorough follow-up and promptness. Nothing came his way.

She browsed through her mailbox on her mobile.

Want to talk to you about our relationship.

You can't deny our love.

Please give our love another chance.

Mrinal can never surpass my love for you.

"Sounds like an appeal from a rejected lover." She reflected aloud.

"He was in love with her. There is no doubt about that--"

"Get Jha to come here in thirty minutes." She cut in.

"But, he is not a suspect anymore. Aren't we closing the case?"

"Tell him that if he doesn't reach in thirty minutes, he will be sitting on the cold floor next to Paul in our lovely lockup." The inspector said calmly.

***

In just under thirty minutes, Virendra Jha was fidgeting on the wooden chair where Paul had sat only days ago.

"I've told you everything." He pleaded defensively.

"Listen to me closely. I'll ask you this, only once." The inspector said in a low voice. "What secret did you share with Rituparna in the school library?"

"I did not share any secret—"

"Do you know what we can do here in this room?" She ran her gaze lazily around the foul-smelling, dimly lit, Spartan room. A chill ran down Jha's spine. The despicable woman was scaring the daylights out of him.

"We can get the truth out of you in many innovative ways." She whispered.

"You have got the murderer. I don't understand, why are you interrogating me? I can get a lawyer to defend—"

"You were the one who told Rituparna Bagdi that she must ask Paul about a secret that you were privy to. That innocent woman followed your instructions. I've reason to believe that the *secret* that she had no clue about triggered Paul to kill her. Hence, we can charge you with abetment." Inspector Roy stood up.

Jha swallowed. His heart was thumping hard against his ribcage. He had never imagined in his wildest dreams that it would come to this. He felt trapped.

"Paul is not what he seems." He breathed unevenly, a few times. "His classmates were scared of him because he knew their secrets. He blackmailed them from time to time. They gave him money to buy his silence."

"How do you know?"

"They confided in me." He smiled uneasily. "I'm not the unpopular ogre you think I am. Kids do love me."

"What else did they tell you that you missed telling us earlier?" She crossed her arms.

He wiped the roof of his mouth with his tongue. "H-he s-sold..." He didn't want to stutter. But, this mouth refused to cooperate. "T-t-t-toffees." He blurted.

"Toffees?"

"He called it toffees. The LSDs and marijuana vapours. Sold it for thousands. He made a lot of money doing that."

She shuddered inside. Her heart pummelled against her chest. "Who was his supplier?" She kept her voice even. She didn't want him to realise that he had given her the missing link. The vital clue.

"I don't know." Jha clicked his tongue. "He sold it to them outside school. Once I caught him selling it to a student right in front of my room. He denied it. You see..." He smiled sardonically. "I'm not Rituparna Bagdi. I saw through his lies. Paul is no genius, but a crook. A drug peddler."

"Virendra Jha." She raised her voice fighting her racing heart. "I give you a choice. You can walk out of this station scot-free and continue to support your family. Or, you can join Paul inside the lockup. What do you want to do?"

Jha gawked in horror. "I-I-I...don't want to be in jail—"

She didn't let him finish. "Good. Then, I presume you're going to testify as a witness."

He shook his head vigorously.

CHAPTER XLVII

The Truth

"Here is Paul's revised confession." SI Das cocked his head at the brown file on the inspector's table as soon as she walked in. An hour ago, when he had rushed in excitedly eager to share about the new development, she wasn't in her room.

Silently, she walked past him carrying a white jute bag. Placing the bag gingerly on the table with one hand, she collapsed on the chair.

"Where were you?"

"At Kalimandir."

"Paul's home?"

She nodded. "I had to retrieve a painting—"

"A painting?"

"We are almost done, Pritam."

"Almost done? I thought this case was closed."

She smiled wearily.

He considered her for a moment. "I don't know why he had lied. He should have come clean with his motive."

"The image of a wronged, misunderstood lover is far superior to that of a cold-blooded killer. Don't you think?"

"The media did lap it up. They started projecting him as the victim—"

"That's exactly what Paul wanted. A twenty-eight-year-old single woman enticed a gullible eighteen-year-old boy. Plus, in court, he might benefit from this projected image. In all probability, it will impact his sentence and lead to a massive reduction of the years spent in jail. After all, he is only a teenager."

"Now, he can't get away—"

She gave him a full smile.

He returned her smile. "You should be happy. You've managed to solve the case in less than two months, with an injured arm."

"Not you. *We*."

SI Das beamed. "Paul wasn't too happy to find me in the interrogation room. He wanted to talk to you."

"How did you manage?"

"I told him that his only way out was to confess. He wasn't convinced. Argued lividly that Lahiri would come to save him because he was his daughter's caretaker. There was no one else to look after that basket case."

She clenched her jaw in fury. "That child is not a basket case. I've seen some of her paintings. She expresses herself through colours, which is a rare talent. Also, Mrs Lahiri has decided to adopt her."

"What? When did that happen?"

"Days ago. She shared the good news when I visited her. Sorry, missed telling you."

"You should have. That would have saved Paul from getting slapped—"

"What? You slapped him? Pritam, you can't do that! This is not how it is done. We must never resort to violence—"

"Well, a few slaps worked like magic. No serious injury. Only a minor bruise on his insolent lips."

She flinched.

He continued. "Gone was the annoying attitude and out came the truth."

"Never, ever, hit anyone in my absence. Understood?" She hissed.

He nodded guiltily.

"All you had to do was mention *toffees* and wait for him to react."

"I did that too. Later. After I had slap—"

She gave him a reproachful look. "Tell me what Paul said. I'm too tired to look through the file." She blinked several times. Her eyelids drooped against her will. It had been one long chase.

"Let me read it out to you." He sprang up, holding the file.

"I'll be back." She blurted leaping up and whizzing past him.

Astonished, he stood there wondering about her sudden disappearance. Minutes later when she scurried back in, her face was wet and her eyes red.

"You washed your face." He murmured.

"Read Paul's confession, please." She commanded sitting ramrod straight on her chair.

Flipping through a few pages, he found the relevant section and began reading with ardour.

She said she knew my secret. From that moment, I stopped trusting her. When she told me later that she didn't, I told her what she was eager to find out. No earth-shattering secret really -- just that I had to sell drugs to make a living and if she cooperated, we could be rich. And have a new life, just us.

I could see that she was afraid of me. Of me? The one who had promised her a new beginning. The only one who acknowledged her brilliance!

She kept on nagging – how it was all wrong and that I should stop. What did she think? She will walk over to the principal's room and warn him about me. Father Joseph didn't listen to her. How could he?

Sunil Lahiri, my weekly drug supplier had paid him a large donation! If news leaked about his collusion with Lahiri, it would tarnish the reputation of his beloved school. And make him look like a fool for giving admission to a boy rescued from a tea stall.

The charity case, Paul!

I knew she would go looking for trouble again. I had to silence her. Told Lahiri as much. But, that moron wouldn't help me. He said we should scare her away. There was no need to kill. I couldn't agree less. If I had let her go, she would have informed the cops. She warned me that she would.

So I went to her home and persuaded her to open the door. I tried drilling some sense. She wouldn't listen. When I hugged her, she fought out of my embrace. The more I tried to calm her down, the more she wrestled and... fell on the floor."

The SI paused. "The rest is as-is. He thought she was dead so he dug a pit and buried her hours later."

The inspector leaped up. Grabbing the jute bag, she made a run for the door.

"Where are we going?" He cried sprinting after her.

"We need to talk to Paul." She darted towards the cell.

***

Paul smiled when he saw the inspector walk in. "We meet again. I knew you wouldn't leave without saying goodbye."

She noticed the bruise on his lips. Without answering, she handed the bag over to the SI.

The SI glared in confusion.

"Take it out."

He took the canvas out of the bag.

"What do you think, Das?" A half-smile played on her lips.

"Not bad." He mumbled.

"Bloody good!" Paul hissed.

The cops ignored him. "You're right, Das. Not bad for an amateur painter. Anything else that you may want to add?"

The SI scanned the painting like an art critic. Tilting his head, raising his chin, scratching his stubble. "This painting looks old...and dirty. Did it fall into a puddle or something—"

"Bingo, Das! Bingo!" She piped up. "It did fall." Her eyes burned with a fire that was blazing inside for days. "Tell us how this beautiful painting was soiled, Paul--"

"This was the only thing left of her. I couldn't let it go. I had hurled it out of anger. I was upset." His lips twitched.

"You went back to her home on 22 November to get the painting. Virendra Jha saw your shadow and Lahiri found you holding *something*. Little did he know that you went to salvage a painting, but didn't save your teacher who was still alive. Writhing and wriggling inside a pit, struggling to come out. Losing her nails in the fray. Why didn't you pull her out?"

"The painting was lying on top of her grave. I did hear her slithering and hissing inside."

"Why didn't you...then?"

"I only wanted the painting back. Not her." He held her gaze.

For the first time, she noticed the flicker of that sinister darkness that peered through his eyes. An esoteric voice whispered in her ears.

There is something feral, animal-like in his stare.

Slowly, she turned away from the piercing gaze of the teenager. The SI followed.

Paul yelled. "Lahiri handed me over to you out of fear. That bastard was not ready to pay me more. I had to threaten him to get a good cut. I was handling his shonky business. Taking care of his dirty secret while he lived in luxury with his family. I deserved a better cut. The scumbag owes me money. So don't go bragging about how you made Lahiri reveal the name of the killer during your interrogation. He wanted me out of his way. I did you a favour—"

The inspector spun around. "You did us a favour, all right. Not in resolving the case but in helping us see who you truly are -- a frightened boy who buried the only person who had appreciated his misplaced genius."

CHAPTER XLVIII

The Diary

"Now, you can use both hands." The doctor laughed hoarsely at his sarcasm.

Jui Roy stood up. Ready to leave. She didn't like the middle-aged doctor or his annoying sense of humour.

"Not so soon." He stopped her with a smile.

For the next fifteen minutes, the doctor made her rotate her wrists clockwise, then anticlockwise. When she surmised he was done, he grinned and made her stretch her left arm several times.

In the beginning, her immobile arm creaked in annoyance. Gradually, it awoke from its month long slumber springing back into action. The pink plaster and sling lay abandoned on the floor of the doctor's clinic.

Jui gazed at her hands feeling like a new person. Being able to use both her limbs made her smile in joy. It was bizarre to feel this happy for something she had taken for granted all her life.

"I've to go." Swiftly, she made her way to the door. She didn't want to be delayed any further.

"Don't they teach inspectors to say, thank you?" The doctor blustered.

Reluctantly she grunted, "Thanks," before scooting off.

***

At the police station, everyone greeted her with a nod at her arm. But, none pointed anything out. No compliment. No observation. They knew better. Pritam Das, however, had no such reservations. As soon as he saw her marching towards her room, without the sling, he bellowed, "Two hands are definitely better than one--”

“Did you call, Mrinal?” She cut in curtly.

“Waiting for you, ma’am.”

Ignoring his jibe, she walked in. A strong scent of cologne hit her nose.

“Inspector.” Mrinal stood up.

“How are you?” She smiled running her eyes over the finest specimen of a man.

“Trying to hold up.” He avoided her gaze.

She walked over to the filing cabinet and removed Rituparna’s diary. “Here. I think you should have this.”

He accepted the long notebook that she held in her outstretched hands. Opening it delicately like a prized possession, he scoured through the pages. When he raised his gaze, his eyes swam in unshed tears. “Thank you, inspector.”

“I hope you don’t mind, I took the liberty of removing the wrapping paper. I want to give it to someone else.”

***

Nights in Agartala sound of insects buzzing synchronously as if in a church choir. Vehicular traffic dies down. The chatter and clanking of neighbours are hushed by sleep. Jui has always been at peace with the silence of the nights, unafraid of its darkness.

Tonight, when she plonked on her bed surrounded by pillows, she did what she does every night. She took out Rituparna’s diary. Not the original, but a photocopy that she had got printed on a Sunday. Opening the bound white papers, she started reading the cursive words, stopping intermittently to admire the curlicue. Suddenly, a thought flashed as clear as lightning.

Not all that’s nurtured blooms.

Rituparna's last entry in which she writes about rose plants but alludes to her favourite student, Paul. This was the clue that had receded to the farthest corner of her mind. Thanks to SP Yadav who had startled her at the water filter during Sunil Lahiri's interrogation.

Turning the bulb on, she put a pillow under her legs and cushioned herself with a few more. An hour later, when she began drifting into the soothing arms of sleep, a bevy of familiar voices vied for her attention.

Smiling, she heard them all.

"I didn't know that she had wrapped her diary with the paper I had gifted her," murmured Dipti teary-eyed clutching the paper closer to her bosom.

"You did well, Roy. Even the CM was impressed." SP Yadav trumpeted in a room filled with uniformed cops. "Also, I've heard that Father Joseph has been replaced. The poor man left for his hometown in Kerela after Paul's confession."

Finally, it was her brother's turn. His voice unlike the rest came from a faraway place accompanied by an astral trill. "It wasn't up to you to save me, Jui Buri...

It never was."

***